"Ah, The Neighbors,"

Connor said. "I'd forgotten what it was like to worry about what the neighbors are thinking."

Maggie didn't like what he was implying. "I suppose you don't have neighbors to worry about, wherever you live."

"Oh, I have them, all right," he replied. "I just don't worry about them."

"Sometimes I think that must be nice," Maggie said with a sigh.

"I thought you said your respectable life appealed to you."

She shot him a quick glance. "Parts of it do," she admitted. "But there are parts I could do without." She didn't want him to ask her which parts she meant, so she added quickly. "I don't suppose you ever get tired of *your* life-style. Being awake when everyone else is asleep, I mean."

Up until last week that life-style had suited him perfectly. But now he was having serious problems with it, and all because of the woman next to him. He tried fiercely to concentrate on something else, but his eyes were constantly distracted by the slight kissable pout of her full lower lip.

Suddenly its seductive charm seemed much more worthwhile than the independent life he'd made for himself.

Dear Reader:

Welcome to Silhouette! What better way to celebrate St. Valentine's Day and all the romance that goes with it than to indulge yourself with a Silhouette Desire?

If this is your first Desire, let me extend an invitation for you to sit back, kick off your shoes and enjoy. If you are a regular reader, you already know what awaits you.

A Silhouette Desire can encompass many varying moods and tones. The books can be deeply emotional and dramatic, or charming and lighthearted. But no matter what, each and every one is a sensual, compelling love story written by and for today's women.

I know you'll enjoy February's *Man of the Month*, *A Loving Spirit* by Annette Broadrick. But I think *all* of the February books are terrific. Give in to Desire . . . you'll be glad you did!

All the best,

Lucia Macro
Senior Editor

Published by Silhouette Books New York

America's Publisher of Contemporary Romance

More Bestsellers from Berkley
The books you've been hearing about and want to read

Bestsellers you've been hearing about—and want to read

CATHRYN CLARE

LOCK, STOCK AND BARREL

SILHOUETTE *Desire*

Published by Silhouette Books New York

America's Publisher of Contemporary Romance

SILHOUETTE BOOKS
300 East 42nd St., New York, N.Y. 10017

ISBN: 0-373-05550-1

First Silhouette Books printing February 1990

Books by Cathryn Clare

Silhouette Desire

To The Highest Bidder #399
Blind Justice #508
Lock, Stock and Barrel #550

CATHRYN CLARE

is a transplanted Canadian who moved south of the border after marrying a far-from-proper Bostonian. She and her husband now live in an old house in central Massachusetts where she divides her time between writing and renovation. ''Three cats and a view of the forest outside my office window help with the writing part,'' she says.

To my mother,
in lieu of a red sports car

One

———

Now there was wet snow running down the back of her neck. Maggie didn't bother reaching up to wipe it away; her gloves were as sodden as the rest of her. In the half hour she'd spent fruitlessly trying to hail a cab, snow seemed to have gotten into every possible nook and cranny, and now she was damp on top of everything else.

She could see her car now, as she crossed the big parking lot outside the international terminal. The roomy four-wheel-drive vehicle was halfway to being a truck, and its roof rose above the other cars. Not that seeing it was going to do her much good, she reflected. She jumped to get across a slushy puddle, and hoped the locksmith would get here as quickly as he'd promised.

This has been the worst day of my life, she thought, and immediately smiled at the exaggeration. She'd had much worse days, when truly catastrophic things had happened. But for sheer volume of little annoying things, this one really took the prize.

Her boots leaked. She curled her toes, and felt them getting wetter and colder. That was the final straw, and for a moment she thought she was going to stop being noble and competent and give in to the powerful desire to burst into tears. Keeping a stiff upper lip was just getting too hard to do.

She was dimly aware of a vehicle coming her way. She turned her head to look, but for a moment she was blinded by the glare of headlights pointed directly at her. In the next instant a dark blue van hurtled past, throwing a spray of slush that drenched Maggie from the toes of her leaky boots all the way to her stiff upper lip.

"Hey!" she yelled, in protest.

To her surprise, the van slowed down, as if the driver had heard her. Then it began to back up, more slowly, although Maggie stepped back out of puddle range, just in case.

The van looked like it had been through the wars. Its fenders were dented, and the scratches and nicks in its paint job proclaimed it to be a seasoned veteran of Boston traffic. But the sign on the driver's door was clear enough: K.C.'s All-Night Locksmith. Maggie glanced at her watch; it was almost exactly 11:30 p.m. She'd give him points for promptness, but that didn't mean she was going to forget the soaking he'd given her.

The driver's window was being rolled down. The man behind the wheel matched the van perfectly, Maggie thought. It wasn't just the battered leather jacket and the rakish grin, either. Something about his heavy black brows, and the strong, humorous line of his mouth gave the impression that this was a man who didn't give a damn what anyone thought of him.

His first words to her proved it. "Messy night, isn't it?" he said. "You look a bit wet."

His casual tone made her angry, and she found that anger was a welcome feeling after the low-grade misery of the day she'd had. "Thanks to you, I'm soaked through," she told him, putting her hands on her hips. "Do you always drive like that?"

"Time is money in my business," he replied, swinging down from the van and banging the door shut behind him. *His* toes clearly weren't getting wet, Maggie thought, not in those rugged work boots. His blue jeans, tucked into the high tops of the boots, looked as well-used as his leather bomber jacket. Locksmiths Maggie had dealt with in the past had all worn uniforms with their names neatly embroidered over the shirt pocket, but maybe when you were the only locksmith willing to come out on a wet March night to unlock a car, you didn't worry about dressing to impress the customers.

He was glancing from her face to a scrap of paper in his hand. His eyes were almost as black as his hair, and there was something unnervingly direct in the way he looked at her. "You wouldn't by any chance be Maggie Lewis, would you?" he asked.

"Believe me, if there was any chance of being someone else today, I think I'd take it," she said, smiling in spite of herself. "But, yes, I'm Maggie Lewis. That's my car over there, and I'm in sort of a rush to get home, so—"

He didn't let her finish. "I'll be as quick as I can," he said, "but first let's just make sure we understand each other. Did my answering service quote you my rates?"

"No. I was so glad to find someone who'd come out that I didn't think to ask." She wrapped her arms around herself, wishing she wasn't so cold and damp.

"I charge eighty dollars an hour, with a one-hour minimum. Now, you mentioned in your message that you have a fancy security system on the car."

"Yes. That's why the police didn't want to bother with it. They suggested I call you."

"I get lots of business that way. The security system may make it a little more difficult to get into the vehicle. And getting the thing going without the key is an extra fifteen."

Maggie did some quick computing. "So it's going to cost me at least ninety-five dollars? That's ridiculous, Mr.—" She paused, wondering what the K.C. stood for.

"My friends call me Connor," he said smoothly. The arrogant son of a gun was still grinning, daring her to be friendly if she could.

She couldn't, not at those rates. "I'll bet you don't charge your friends ninety-five dollars to get their cars going, or they'd be calling you something else entirely," she said. She heard the icy politeness in her voice.

Those impossibly dark brown eyes seemed to note her consternation. His grin broadened a little. "Well, like it or not, those are my rates," he told her. "Now, how are you planning to pay me?"

"Wait a minute." She held up a gloved hand. "I haven't even said I'm going to hire you, yet. There's no need to talk about paying you until after you've done the work, is there?"

"Ms. Lewis—"

"It's Mrs., actually." There it was, that echo of the ultrarespectable world she'd worked so hard to fit into. *I'm sounding like my mother-in-law*, she thought wryly. Why should one pair of laughing brown eyes make her feel so defensive about her entire life-style?

"Mrs. Lewis, then. Let me tell you a sad story—and a brief one, because I've got three other calls waiting for me, and if you don't want to hire me, I don't have time to waste here." He leaned against the door of his van, oblivious to the water streaming down its sides. Maggie could sense strength in his crossed forearms, and utter independence in the way he tilted his handsome head toward her.

"I've been in this business for almost ten years," he said. "And at first I used to believe every hard-luck story I heard. You know, I lost my keys, I've been mugged, my husband changed the locks and didn't tell me."

"Those don't sound so unbelievable to me," she countered.

"Oh, they were mostly believable enough. It's just that whenever I got to feeling sorry for someone, and told them they could pay me when they had a chance to get to the bank on Monday, I'd find myself out a hundred bucks, or chasing a customer for weeks to get paid for my work."

"I can guarantee you that won't happen with me."

"You can guarantee it all you want, but that doesn't put the money in my pocket. I know this sounds pretty cynical, Mrs. Lewis, but I can guarantee *you* that I couldn't run my business if I trusted every stranger who calls me up to unlock a door."

"It does sound pretty cynical," she replied. "What do you do when you meet someone who's had her purse stolen with her keys in it? Because that's just what happened to me."

"I give them a dime, out of the goodness of my heart, and suggest they call a friend to come and get them." He wasn't budging an inch.

"I can't do that," Maggie said. She was making her voice extra-firm, to keep any suspicious quavers out of it. After all she'd been through today, it was the last straw to have her supposed rescuer give her such a hard time. "It's almost midnight, in case you hadn't noticed, and all the people I can think of to call will be in bed by now."

He cocked a black eyebrow at her, and she could almost hear his mocking thoughts. No doubt a woman whose entire circle of friends went to bed before midnight seemed pretty tame to an all-night rogue like this one.

"Anyway," she went on, "I did try getting a cab, to take me to my mother-in-law's house. But a couple of international flights just got in, plus it's the end of school break and the whole airport is mobbed with students. The cabs are all taking double and triple loads, and no one was going in my direction."

"Where do you live?"

"Wellesley," she said, naming one of Boston's more distant suburban towns.

He snorted—contemptuously, it sounded like. "The original place you can't get to from anywhere," he said. "Well, Mrs. Lewis, I agree you're in a tough spot, but that doesn't mean I'm bending my rules. Do you want me to unlock your car for you, and if so, how are you going to pay me?"

Maggie shoved her hands deep into her pockets, and glanced at her car. It was so close—and so inaccessible. All she wanted at the moment was to climb into the driver's seat and get out of here, away from the slushy puddles and Connor's challenging grin.

"Yes, I want you to unlock it," she said, "and there's only one way I can pay you, if you insist on being paid tonight. I keep a blank check in the glove compartment, for emergencies. Will that do?"

"Sorry, it won't."

It was getting harder and harder to keep from sounding as dispirited as she felt. "What?" she demanded, knowing that quaver would take over her voice before long. "Don't tell me you don't take checks."

"Checks bounce," he said laconically. "I take cash, and I take credit cards."

"That's completely unreasonable!"

That maddening smile broadened again. "I nearly went out of business being reasonable," he said, brushing his thick black hair back from his forehead. "I'm sorry my answering service didn't warn you about this. They're supposed to let people know my policies before I show up, to weed out the—" He paused.

"The deadbeats, I suppose," Maggie finished. "Do I look like a deadbeat to you?"

His pause lengthened, and Maggie wished she could withdraw the question. He was looking intently at her, seeming to assess exactly what she *did* look like, and something in those dark eyes made her feel he was coming entirely too close to the truth.

"Why don't you call your husband to come and get you?" he asked.

The question caught her off guard, with an unexpected sting. A dozen times today she'd wished for Grant's dependable shoulder to lean on, to make this awful day seem a little bit better. She'd come to terms with widowhood in the past five years, but being reminded of it by this cocky stranger was the last thing she needed.

"Why don't you mind your own business?" she returned sharply, and saw his eyes narrow in surprise. The Wellesley-matron pose she'd been using was fading fast, replaced by something much closer to the real Maggie Lewis.

"Now wait a minute," he began, but she cut him off.

"I don't want to wait a minute," she said, "and you've already pointed out how busy you are, so let's get this over with. All I want to do is get home and go to bed. It's been a hell of a day." She still refused to let her voice wobble, and the anger Connor had stirred up helped her resolve. "I have a single check to my name at the moment—a perfectly good check that won't bounce—and that's what I'll pay your ridiculous rates with, if you'll agree. If you won't, we're both wasting our time. Now what do you say?"

It annoyed her to see he'd started grinning again, as if he were enjoying her sudden flash of temper. "I'll tell you what," he said. "I happen to be having an end-of-the-month special on car doors. I'll unlock it and get the thing going for eighty bucks. All right?"

"And the check?"

He sighed, still looking bemused. "It goes against my better judgment, but you really do look like you've had a hell of a day. I'll take the check, and it had better not be rubber."

"It's not," she said hastily. She could feel her resolve caving in on her, now that the prospect of home and bed were becoming realities. "Please hurry, Mr....Connor. I'm going to be dead on my feet if this day goes on much longer."

He pushed himself away from his van door in a fluid motion that hinted of well-developed muscles. "No need for that," he said. "Why don't you sit in the van while I do the work?" He hoisted himself into the driver's seat and opened the passenger door from the inside. Gratefully, Maggie climbed in.

Connor was reaching into the back of the van, twisted around between the bucket seats so that his broad upper body was very close to her. He was a hard man to ignore, Maggie thought, and wondered whether it was just images of crying on Grant's sympathetic shoulder that was making Connor's nearness so appealing.

"Here," he said finally, turning to face her. "This towel's seen better days, I'm afraid, but it's better than nothing. You look soaked to the skin."

"And beyond." She couldn't help smiling. She raised her eyes to meet his and saw something very surprising. He'd worn that cocky grin the whole time they were negotiating, while she'd been aloof and then angry. Now that she was smiling at him, his grin was gone. He looked dead serious, for some reason.

"We can't have that," he said. His forceful voice had become not much more than a husky murmur. He leaned over in his seat and ran the towel gently along the side of her face. She could feel the warmth of his hands.

It wasn't just a friendly gesture, and Maggie responded to it immediately. There was something potent in the way he was looking at her, and as she settled back into the bucket seat and let him brush the melted snow from her face and hair, she could feel her heart rate starting to pick up speed, prompted by the muscular gentleness of the man beside her.

The man who hadn't even introduced himself fully, she reminded herself. The man she knew nothing about, except that he was supposed to be unlocking her car so she could get out of here. It was crazy to let herself respond this way, just because she'd had a tough day and it was so comforting to have someone pampering her, even a little bit.

She had to do something to get things back on a more normal footing. "Do you get all your towels from the Ritz?" she asked him, nodding at the telltale logo on the somewhat frayed white towel.

His grin came back, not abashed at all. "If I could afford to stay at the Ritz, I wouldn't have to worry about stealing towels," he said. "This one was left in my van by some guy who needed his front door opened. He *could* afford to stay at the Ritz, too. It beats me why rich people can be so stingy about little things."

The way he said "rich people" had a bitter sound to it. Maggie was silent, feeling the divided loyalty that always bothered her when the subject of wealth came up. If having money made you a rich person, then she was one, and a part of her was stung by Connor's blanket statement about the stinginess of rich people. But a part of her had never been comfortable with the wealthy surroundings she'd married into. Maybe it was that part that found Connor's obvious bohemianism so attractive.

Her comment about the towel had at least defused that attraction a bit, as she'd intended it to. Connor was handing her the towel now, sliding agilely into the back of the van as he dug—for tools she assumed—in the surprisingly organized clutter. He seemed almost relieved that she'd lightened the mood between them.

"I won't be long," he told her, opening the van's back doors and dropping down onto the wet pavement as though making an escape. "You'll be writing out that check in half an hour."

Eighty dollars for half an hour's work was a bit steep, she thought. She could hear his heavy-soled work boots on the pavement as he headed for her car and realized, with a start, that this was the first time she'd been by herself since Jordan had called to her sometime just before dawn this morning. *Yesterday* morning, she corrected, glancing at her watch and noting that midnight had already come and gone.

And then, try as she might tell herself that all days were not like this, that she'd gotten used to being a widow and a single mother, that she didn't care if her toes were wet, that Connor's vagabond good looks hadn't stirred her in places that made her feel very vulnerable indeed, those thoughts came rushing in with the dreary insistence of the wet snow dripping down the windshield in front of her.

If Connor hadn't touched her so gently and then left so abruptly, she might have been able to go on keeping a stiff upper lip for another hour or so. But not now. She leaned forward in her seat, forehead on her cold fingertips, and let the wave of self-pity she'd been fighting off all day roll right over her.

Connor Blake didn't usually whistle while he worked. Usually he kept up a muttered commentary under his breath, as though he could bully or coerce the mechanism into doing what he wanted. But tonight he found himself whistling.

He knew why, and it was damned unsettling. Ever since he'd started this crazy one-man business, he'd had an equally crazy fantasy that some dark night, on a routine call, he'd meet a woman who could jolt him out of the independent routine he'd made for himself, a woman who could balance and complete all the things he knew were missing in his life. He'd had no clear idea of what that woman would look like—until tonight. Now he knew she looked like Maggie Lewis.

Not that he could have described Maggie in any detail, he thought, whistling an old school football fight song. He couldn't tell what color her hair was, since it was half-soaked with wet snow. She was of medium height—five-feet-eight or so—but her figure was well-bundled up in a conservative tan trench coat. It was only her eyes that had captured and held him.

Ah, yes, those eyes. He could describe *them* minutely. A deep, liquid gold at the center, with hazel edges. And they'd looked at him with an independent gleam that he liked very much.

He sat back on his heels for a moment, pausing in mid-phrase of the fight song he thought he'd forgotten. The fantasy of his perfect woman was going to stay just that—a fantasy—and he knew it. Maggie Lewis was married, and had been quick to point it out. And anyway, she would probably turn out to be nothing more than the well-to-do Wellesley wife and mother she'd come across as at first. He'd had enough of that type to last him a lifetime.

It was just that when she'd showed that flash of temper, he thought he'd glimpsed something more elemental in her character, something that called powerfully to him. Connor sighed and started whistling again. It didn't do to mix fantasy with reality, he knew. He'd keep the fantasy of Maggie Lewis's gold-and-hazel eyes, and not get any further into it than that.

That was easy enough to say—until he finished unlocking her car and returned to his van to find her crying in the front seat.

She was being subtle about it, but he could see traces of tears on her lashes. The curve of her shoulders told him how tired and depressed she was feeling. She looked up as he opened the door, hastily rubbing her eyes with the towel she still held.

"I'm almost dry," she said, with a smile that was manufactured for his benefit. "Is the car unlocked?"

"Unlocked, but not started yet," he replied. "I just came back to get some more tools—and to see how you were getting along." He couldn't resist adding that.

Her gold eyes widened, drawing him further into their magic. "Is that part of the service?" she wondered out loud. "I thought you had three other customers waiting for you."

He did, but a man didn't get an opportunity to indulge a fantasy every day. He wasn't going to rush this one. "They aren't urgent," he hedged. "And you look like you need help with more than just your car."

She seemed to be considering whether to confide in him, as he was offering. "It's nothing a good night's sleep won't fix," she said finally, with a smile just as wan as the last one had been. "My son woke me up at a really ungodly hour this morning, and things have been going downhill ever since."

"How old is your son?" he asked, to keep the conversation going.

"Seven." Her smile strengthened. "Going on forty, I sometimes think. He looks after me as much as I look after him. The only time he really seems like a child is when he's sick—and he's been sick all week. He had a coughing fit at 5:00 a.m., and refused to go back to sleep until I came and sat by his bed." The smile became self-deprecating. "I'm sure you don't need to listen to my domestic problems, Mr....Connor."

"I don't mind, at all."

She was watching him closely, and he felt himself basking in the warmth of that gaze. Suddenly, finding out everything about her seemed to be the most important thing in the world.

"What went wrong after that?" he asked, leaning a little closer. Her hair was starting to dry now, he noticed, and it framed her face in a curling, shoulder-length mane. It was a tawny color, with gold highlights, matching her eyes perfectly. She reminded him of a lioness that someone had managed to domesticate—almost.

"Oh, Lord. I don't know where to start. I've been fighting off Jordan's cold myself, for one thing. And because he's been home from school, it makes it harder for me to concentrate on the other kids."

"You have more children?"

"No. I run a day-care center in my house."

That surprised him. Here he'd been picturing her as a well-off young matron, not a working woman.

"I have six kids most days," she went on. "And one of the little ones picked today to fall and hit her head on the corner of a table." She made a wry face. "Thank goodness she didn't really hurt herself, but she cut her forehead open and there was a lot of blood. The older kids came up with the gruesome theory that she had a hole in her head and her brains were going to fall out on the floor.'' Her full lips twisted into a reluctant smile. "I work alone until three o'clock, when I have some teenage girls come in to help out. So I had to load all seven of the kids into the car to take little Natasha to the doctor. It was quite an adventure.''

"I can believe that," Connor said. "In my experience, getting *one* kid ready to go anywhere is quite an adventure.''

"You're right.'' She seemed to appreciate his understanding. Her words were spilling out now, as if she'd been waiting all day for someone to listen to her misadventures. "Well, I'll spare you the rest of the gory details, but Natasha ended up with four stitches in her head, plus I had to deal with her hysterical mother who didn't help things, at all. *I* ended up with a bad headache and no time to cook dinner, and then my regular baby-sitter got sick with the same bug Jordan's got, so I had to take him to his grandmother's house while I drove to the airport.'' She sighed. "I just hope to heaven she doesn't get his cold, too. The poor woman has had enough to cope with recently.''

"I suppose you were dropping your husband off at the airport,'' Connor said casually, making it into a question.

"No.'' The flow of words stopped abruptly, and she turned those wide eyes away from him. "My sister-in-law, actually.''

Connor frowned. Fantasy or not, he was getting more and more curious about this woman. Maybe she was divorced, or maybe her marriage wasn't a happy one. She'd been voluble enough about her son, but she'd closed up tight at the mention of a husband.

"And then your purse got stolen,'' he prompted.

She looked sideways at him, and seemed to decide to go on. "Oh, there's more yet,'' she said. "I was in such a hurry to get here on time that I drove faster than I usually do, and

I got a ticket for speeding. Would you believe I've never gotten a ticket before? Not even for parking.''

"I get parking tickets all the time," he said, "and believe me, you haven't been missing anything. What else happened?"

"Oh, that's about it. I saw my sister-in-law off, and was on my way to call my mother-in-law to tell her I'd be late, when I got stuck in the middle of a crowd coming off an international flight. When I got out of the crush, my purse was gone." She spread her hands, now gloveless, in a palms-up gesture. "And that's about it, except for getting splashed by your van and finding out it's going to cost me eighty dollars to get home."

Her fingers were long and slender, and they looked very cold. Connor tried to hang onto the last shreds of normalcy, and to tell himself he should be starting her car for her and then getting on with the rest of his night's work. But Maggie Lewis drew him too strongly.

Before she'd even finished speaking, he reached out a hand and captured one of hers. Her fingers were as icy as they looked, and the instant he touched her he knew he wanted to warm all of her and take away the harried look in her eyes.

"You still feel half-frozen," he commented, and reached with his free hand to the key that was still in the ignition. "If I'd been thinking, I would have left the heat on for you."

Almost immediately Maggie could feel the temperature inside the van starting to rise, and she knew only part of it was due to the heater. She was astonished by how good it felt to be touched by Connor. Just having him hold her hand like this made her feel as though the rest of the day had been in black-and-white, and now suddenly someone had turned on the technicolor.

"I'm all right," she said, hoping madly that her feelings weren't on display. "I actually feel much better now that I've told you the whole sad story."

"Well, as I said, I've had lots of experience listening to sad stories." His grin didn't seem quite so cocky now, and Maggie wondered if he, too, was feeling some stirrings inside him. He slid his thumb along her palm, and she heard her heartbeat jump in response.

There was a silence that seemed long, and then Connor said, "I would have thought your husband would help you out with a rough day like this one." He sounded as if he hadn't really wanted to say the words, but hadn't quite been able to keep them in.

"I'm sure he would have," Maggie said evenly, "but he's not around. He died five years ago."

She couldn't read the look that crossed his face. "I see," he said, nodding slowly. "I'm sorry."

"Thanks," she said simply. "I've gotten used to it—most of the time. It's just that on days like this . . ."

She didn't finish the sentence. Their eyes were locked together now, and she felt herself being drawn into those velvety, near-black depths. This mysterious man seemed to hold something out to her, some promise of what had been lacking up till now, and she felt herself going willingly toward it, not stopping to think.

Connor heard her sharp intake of breath as he reached for her, but the only thing that moved was her mouth. Her lips parted slightly, responding in a way he couldn't gauge, and her look of uncertain expectancy was driving him wild. He was thinking inescapably of those soft lips, and the welcoming darkness within.

To keep his mind from racing too far out of control, he tightened his grip on her fingers, and was astonished to feel her gripping him in return. This was just a fantasy, he reminded himself forcibly. Whatever was happening here was only for the moment. But for the moment, he was as caught up in it as he'd ever been in anything.

"I think I must be imagining this," she said, echoing his thoughts exactly. Her voice was slightly breathy, softer than it had been. "All day I've been wishing for a pair of broad shoulders to cry on—and now you've materialized out of nowhere.''

''My shoulders and I are at your service,'' he said. He sounded a little husky-voiced himself. ''You can cry on them if you like.''

Their hands were still locked together, as though neither of them could quite decide where to go from here. Connor knew there was no reasonable direction for this to lead, but he couldn't let her go and return to the world of reason quite yet. He leaned forward, drawn by something outside his own will, and kissed her.

Maggie found herself caught up in something much more than mere comfort. His mouth covered hers persuasively, knowingly, as though they were such total strangers that they could afford to be completely open. She welcomed the searching of his tongue, and parted her lips to make his tender exploration more complete. The instant she felt their mouths merge so intimately, reason went away and pure sensation took over.

His tongue moved around hers in a pulsating pattern that never slackened until a moan of buried passion sounded deep in her throat. He clasped her to him, and she could feel the warmth of his fingers through her still-damp hair. Without meaning to, she raised her own hands and ran them through the jet black strands at the base of his neck. His battered leather jacket felt rough under her fingertips, and the image of his mocking grin flashed through her mind.

That was what she was responding to, she knew. The vagabond who'd appeared out of the night. The stranger she would never see again, whose dark eyes stirred her so powerfully. The freedom in Connor's whole bearing.

That freedom lasted precisely as long as his kiss. When he raised his head again, Maggie knew she couldn't possibly go any further with this. She took in a deep breath, fighting to get her pounding pulse under control as she disentangled her fingers from his.

"I really think I should be getting home," she said. She looked out the van window at her car, as if it could give her some reassurance that the world was still the way it had been half an hour ago, before Connor had tilted things upside down with his kindness and his kiss.

"You're probably right." He seemed taken aback by their shared instant of passion, and glad to turn his attention back to the saner world of locks and tools. "I'll get the engine going, and you can write out that check in your glove compartment. Just make it out to K.C.'s All-Night Locksmith."

Maggie hopped down from the passenger seat, avoiding a puddle, and followed Connor to her car. She traced a finger along the side of his van on the way, underlining the logo with his business name painted on the dark blue vehicle.

"How long did you say you'd been in business?" she asked him.

"About ten years. Why?"

"I just wondered. This poor old van looks like it's been with you from the beginning."

"Believe it or not, I started out using a motorcycle. I only bought the van when my toolbox got too big for the bike." His grin reappeared, transforming his handsome face. "And this poor old van is good for another hundred-thousand miles, at least. It's just the surface that's a bit banged up. We're alike in that way."

He stopped in front of her car, hands on his hips and that mocking smile dancing in his eyes. He was right, Maggie thought. His face, with its cynicism one moment and its impossible tenderness the next, had been places and seen things. As she'd once hoped to do, before wealth and marriage and respectability had put their stamp on her.

Well, this chance encounter with Connor would just be filed in her memory as a small but potent reminder of what Maggie might have been, she decided, amused at her own philosophizing. She got into her car as Connor flipped up the hood, and by the time he had mysteriously started the engine, she had a check ready for him.

He took it, not bothering to glance at it as he explained to her how to turn the engine off when she got home, and how to go about getting a new key cut for the ignition. She felt a strange reluctance to say goodbye to him, and from the intensity of his gaze, she thought he seemed to be feeling the same thing.

"It's funny," she said, looking up at him. "I don't even know your last name."

"Most people don't. I don't use it much." His rakish grin tilted up a few degrees.

"Do you like . . . doing this for a living?"

"Sure. It suits me. Crazy hours, a completely unpredictable job, and no boss looking over my shoulder."

She could believe that. Everything about him said "free spirit" in letters ten feet high. "You're lucky," she said. "Most people aren't nearly so satisfied with their jobs."

"Luck has nothing to do with it. I wasn't satisfied with the way I was before, so I changed things." It sounded so simple, Maggie thought, knowing that nothing was ever quite that simple. "What about you? Aren't you satisfied with what you do?"

She shrugged, and suddenly she wanted the conversation to be done. He was getting too close to things she didn't usually let herself think about, and with that cussed honesty of his, he'd be hauling out her deepest secrets in no time if she let him. She was glad she'd encountered him and still warmed inside at the memory of his kiss, but she didn't want to go any further than that.

"Most days, yes," she said lightly. "It's only sore throats and speeding tickets and pickpockets that put the edge on things, occasionally. Thanks so much for your help, Connor, and—" She was starting to frame an awkward thank-you for the use of his shoulder to cry on, when she saw him glance down at the check she'd handed him. When he looked back up, his face had changed utterly.

The grin was gone. So was the openness she'd found so appealing. He looked somehow older, harder.

"All in the line of business," he said, with no humor at all. "Assuming this check is as good as you say, you won't be seeing me again. Try keeping your keys in your coat pocket from now on. That way, you can at least get home on your own."

He seemed to be trying to undo all the friendly feelings he'd encouraged between them. The expression in his eyes seemed to say that if she'd had the sense to keep her keys in her pocket before now, he wouldn't have had to bother coming out to rescue her.

Maggie was stung by the change in him. *I might have known nothing good was going to happen today,* she thought miserably. She had no interest in trying to find out what had gone wrong. A quick trip home and a good night's sleep were what she'd been craving all evening, and she turned her thoughts back in that direction as though she could forget that Connor whatever-his-name-was even existed. Her goodbye, as she got into her car, was brief and to the point.

Connor watched her drive away, kicking himself mentally for being such a damn fool. When he couldn't see the red taillights of her car any more he took another look at the check in his hand, shielding it from the wet snow that was still falling. It said the same thing as the first time he'd looked: Mrs. Grant A. Lewis, Jr.

Grant's widow. Of all the women in the world, his fantasy had turned out to be a central part of the world Connor had been running full-tilt away from most of his adult life.

With an angry growl, Connor stalked back to his van. He'd let himself be carried away by the independent shine in a pair of gold-and-hazel eyes, and all the time she had been one of the Lewis clan, and more than likely a major force in the family company. Connor's father would have a good belly laugh at that one, Connor thought bitterly. The old man was always claiming loudly that Connor couldn't escape his destiny forever.

"I can and I will," he muttered savagely, putting the van into gear and splashing through the puddles on his way out of the parking lot.

He was halfway through his next job—replacing the lock on a corner variety store that had been broken into—before he recovered some of the amused detachment he prided himself on. It took some willpower, but he managed to force his mind onto the bolts and barrels of the lock he was working on, and away from thoughts of how it had felt to kiss Maggie Lewis.

Even so, this time he wasn't whistling.

TWO

March had certainly gone out like a lion, Connor thought, but it didn't seem to be completely gone yet. It was a week after his meeting with Maggie, and he was standing on her doorstep in Wellesley, with his collar turned up against the early April gale that was blowing around him.

The house was exactly the kind of place he could picture Grant Lewis buying. It was a solid two-story brick building, roomy without being pretentious. The grounds were carefully landscaped with trees and shrubs, and the whole place had an air of wealthy respectability.

That had been Grant all over, Connor thought. Steady and dependable. Maybe it had been an attraction of opposites that had made Grant and Connor such good friends as boys. He found himself wondering whether Grant, too, had caught that flash of fire in Maggie's eyes and been attracted by it.

Then he made himself stop thinking about Maggie's eyes. That wasn't, after all, why he was here. He fingered the check in his pocket and reached out to push the doorbell.

The door was opened in thirty seconds by Little Lord Fauntleroy.

Connor blinked, as though the small apparition might disappear. But the boy who was regarding him with a level stare was obviously real, and after he'd gotten past the Edwardian costume—velvet knickers and a loose white shirt with a floppy bow at the neck—Connor knew exactly who the child was. It was uncannily like stepping back in time and seeing his own childhood companion again.

"Is your mother at home?" he asked Grant's son. The boy nodded.

"She's in the playroom," he said, "but she's busy. Can you wait a few minutes?"

"Sure." Connor stepped into the large, brick-tiled foyer and watched the boy closing the door behind him like a scaled-down footman. "You're Jordan, aren't you?"

"Yes." The round brown eyes looked surprised. "How did you know?"

Connor grinned at him. "Just a lucky guess," he said.

Jordan clearly wasn't comfortable with having his leg pulled, Connor thought. Just like his father had been.

"Why don't you come and sit in the living room?" the boy suggested, leading the way across the foyer. His small black patent-leather shoes echoed loudly on the tile. "I expect you're wondering why I'm dressed like this," he said over his shoulder.

"I have to admit the thought did cross my mind," Connor said, amused.

"It's for the school play," Jordan explained. "I'm playing The Little Prince."

"Where do you go to school?" Connor thought he could guess.

"The Stearns School. It's in Newton."

"I know where it is." There was very little Connor didn't know about it, having gone to the exclusive private school himself. "Do you like it?"

Jordan shrugged, the first wholly childlike gesture Connor had seen him make. "It's okay," he said. "My father went there, and my grandfather, so I guess they thought I should go there, too."

"Parents often think things like that," Connor said soberly. He wished Maggie's small son didn't stir up so many echoes of the past—not to mention some all-too-recent ones.

Jordan was nodding vigorously. "Parents are very big on tradition," he agreed, as though it was a mystery he'd learned to accept in his seven years.

"What about your mother?" Connor couldn't help asking. "Is she big on tradition, too?"

Jordan considered it. "Sometimes she is, and sometimes she isn't," was his final pronouncement. "I'll go and tell her you're here."

He pattered out through the foyer and Connor stepped into the carpeted, low-ceilinged room, with its exposed beams and large brick fireplace. It was a comfortable room, with built-in bookcases and low leather sofas. The late-afternoon light slanted in through leaded-glass windows and warmed the oak of the paneled walls. Here and there Connor spotted small racing cars and dinosaur models. He smiled to himself. His own mother had strictly forbidden toys in the living room.

Then his smile faded, because in all other particulars the house reminded him so precisely of the place where he'd grown up. He'd spent far too many of his boyhood hours in a living room much like this one, being bored while his parents and Grant's had discussed the social world and the endless business of Triple I.

Just the thought of that damned company made him want to bolt for the front door. He tried to make himself comfortable in one of the leather chairs, but after a few seconds he stood as though the chair's seat had been spiked.

It was no good. He'd made his escape from this comfortable, wealthy setting years ago, and he couldn't be at home here any longer. He strode through the foyer toward the sound of voices coming from the back of the house, determined to finish his business with Maggie and get out as soon as he could.

Maggie was beginning to think the phrase "Thank God it's Friday" was way off the mark. Last Friday had been an utter disaster, starting with Jordan's bad cold and ending with Connor's unexplained rejection, and this Friday hadn't been much better.

Well, she was starting to get things straightened out now, thank goodness. All but one of her day-care kids had been picked up, and once she'd paid her afternoon baby-sitters she would be free to get dinner ready and get Jordan back to the school for the play tonight. Light at the end of the tunnel, she thought, opening her checkbook.

"I'm sorry to keep you waiting, Lisa," she said to the blond teenager in front of her. "I'm beginning to think I'm going to have to start charging extra for parents who don't pick up their kids on time."

"That's all right, Mrs. Lewis," Lisa said. "As long as Sherry and I get a cut."

The two girls giggled, and Maggie smiled at them. She was lucky to have these two, she knew. They were reliable, and good with the kids. She handed Lisa her paycheck and started to write out Sherry's.

"Better make sure those checks are good, ladies," said a voice behind her, and Maggie turned quickly, bitten by the unpleasant tone even before she'd identified the speaker.

Then she felt her brows draw together in an involuntary frown as she recognized Connor. Her first thought was that he looked ridiculously out of place. The playroom was decorated for children, with bright colors and simple shapes. In his beat-up leather jacket and heavy boots, not to mention his threatening dark eyes, Connor looked like a black thundercloud in the middle of a sunny afternoon. Even more than his dark coloring, his aggressive maleness seemed to jar with the cozy setting Maggie had created.

"What do you mean?" she demanded, setting her pen down.

He produced a slip of paper from his jacket pocket and waved it at her. It was the check she'd written him last Friday night, she realized, and it was rubber-stamped repeatedly. She could see that it had been refused due to insufficient funds.

"I mean," he said slowly, heavily, "that your check turned out to be rubber, in spite of your personal guarantee. I just thought I should warn these ladies that their paychecks may not be good."

"In the first place, these are not 'ladies.' They are young women," she informed him, feeling her temper rising. "In the second place, their paychecks are perfectly good, since I just balanced my business account last night. And in the third place—"

There was a knock at the door, and Maggie turned to the two girls, who were watching the exchange with wide eyes. "That'll be Karl's mother," she said. "Could you get him ready? Thanks."

"What's the third place?" Connor demanded, as the girls turned their attention to a child in a playpen.

"In the third place, you have absolutely no business barging in here and making unfounded accusations about me in front of my employees." What was happening here? Maggie wondered. She made it a rule never to lose her temper. It had been drilled into her that that was one of the things a well-bred young woman simply did not do. And Connor the locksmith, in two encounters, had brought her once-fearsome temper to the surface twice. "How did you get in, anyway?"

"Not by barging," he said, seeming amused by her anger. "Your son let me in. And I'd hardly call this an unfounded accusation. The check did bounce, after all."

"I can see that, and if you'll give me two minutes to finish up here, I'll do something about it," she told him. She wasn't quite her usual calm self as she finished writing out Sherry's paycheck and saw the two baby-sitters and Karl's mother to the door, and that annoyed her even further. It was bad enough for Connor to try to catch her off guard like this. But even worse, he seemed to have succeeded.

Connor was losing his own private battle to stay calm and detached. Being here was simply stirring up too many things for him: memories of Grant, thoughts of the still-unresolved battle with his father over Triple I, and the same powerful longing to get closer to Maggie Lewis that he'd succumbed to a week ago.

She was even lovelier than he remembered, now that her thick brown hair was dry and framing her face in gentle waves. She was wearing a pair of dark brown pants tailored to fit a very trim figure, and a loose-fitting gold cotton sweater that matched her eyes.

Her eyes were the same, and they'd been haunting Connor all week.

She seemed to be deliberately taking her time saying her goodbyes, making him wait. Connor settled himself on a pint-sized chair, putting his feet up on a small table, and watched her making a conscious effort to calm herself down.

When she turned to face him again, that well-bred veneer was almost all back in place—until she saw where he was. "That furniture was just repainted," she informed him crisply. "I'd appreciate it if you'd take your boots off it."

"You didn't offer me a seat," he replied, "so I thought I'd help myself."

"You seem to make a habit of helping yourself to things," she shot back, and he knew she was thinking of their kiss last Friday night. She didn't blush. Her almost-olive complexion wouldn't give her away that way, he thought, but her confusion was evident on her face. Good.

"Why don't you come into my office, and I'll see if I can figure out where the mistake is?" She led the way to a small room at one end of the large playroom, and Connor followed her, swinging his long legs down from the table. The office was as tastefully decorated as the rest of the place, with a small oak desk, tan filing cabinets and simple white blinds on the windows. Correct. Proper. Elegant.

Connor was feeling his usual reaction to correctness and elegance. They made him want to throw things, or run away. He clenched his teeth and sat down in the chair Maggie offered him, and waited while she sorted through a stack of envelopes on the desk.

"My bank statement came today, but I haven't had a chance to do anything about it yet," she told him, neatly slitting open an envelope with a letter-opener. Connor opened his mail by sticking a thumb in one corner and ripping the envelope to shreds.

He watched her as she perused the computer-printed statement, and tried to come to grips with his conflicting feelings. On the one hand, he wanted to cut and run for it. Maybe he was right about her, and there were other hidden layers beneath this proper, businesslike one. But even so, getting involved with her would have to lead him straight back into the life he'd gotten away from.

He'd almost forgotten the bounced check by the time she spoke again. "Damn," she said forcefully, striking the sheet of paper with the letter opener. "I think it's a computer error. I sent in a check for Jordan's tuition last month, and they seemed to have entered it twice." She reached for the white phone on the desk and dialed a number from memory. "It's just four-thirty. If we're quick, we can get to the bank before five and sort this out."

"What do you mean, we? This is your problem, not mine."

"This is the fastest way to get you your money. That's what you want, isn't it?" Her eyes seemed to throw sparks at him, and he almost regretted his heavy-handed approach.

She was speaking into the phone now. "This is Mrs. Grant Lewis," she said, and Connor winced. That was who she was, after all, not some mystery woman he'd conjured up out of a dream. She was as solidly rooted in the world of Triple I as he'd once been.

From the rapidity of the way she was transferred to the bank manager, a lot of other people were aware of that fact. Maggie explained the problem to the manager, accepted his apologies graciously, and arranged to come by the bank immediately to straighten things out.

"If you can spare half an hour to come with me, I'll be able to give you cash," she said, hanging up the phone. "Will that suit you, Mr.—" She paused, and frowned. "What *is* your last name, anyway?"

"I told you, I don't use it much."

"Why not?"

"It's not a name I particularly like."

"Well, I guess that's your business. Are you coming to the bank, or not?"

"Sure. Don't most banks close at three or four?"

"This one does, too. But I happen to be acquainted with the manager. He's in his office until five, and he's usually very nice about helping out when there's a problem."

"How do you know the bank manager so well?" He was challenging her, she thought, and couldn't imagine why.

"I inherited a substantial share in my husband's family's business," she told him. "It includes a seat on the board of directors. Our bank manager is also on the board, so I see him frequently."

She could tell she was sounding prim again, the echoes of the conservative, wealthy world were starting to crop up in her speech. She didn't know why Connor did that to her, or why he seemed so interested in her life.

She was still frowning as she collected her purse and headed toward the front door. Try as she might to put Connor out of her mind entirely, she'd found herself thinking about him all week, and one of the most mysterious things about him was his insistence on using only his first name. She'd come up with an unsettling theory: anyone who could pick locks legally could also do it illegally, and she wondered if a criminal record might be what Connor was hiding so assiduously. Could his questions about her financial dealings possibly have anything to do with that?

"Jordan?" she called up the stairs, as she took her tan trench coat from the front hall cupboard. "Grab your coat, honey. We have to go to the bank."

"Can't I stay here, Mom?" the boy's voice came back. "I'm practicing my lines."

"It'll only take half an hour," she promised. "You know I don't like to leave you alone."

Grudgingly, Jordan came down the wide, carpeted staircase, still wearing his Little Lord Fauntleroy costume. "*He* could stay with me," he suggested, pointing to Connor.

"No, he couldn't. He's the reason we need to go to the bank. Don't you want to take off that bow, honey? It'll get crushed."

"No way." Jordan smiled broadly. "I want to see what Mr. Dennis says when he sees my outfit." He ran back upstairs in search of his coat.

"Oh, Lord." Maggie couldn't repress a smile as she glanced at Connor. "I seem to be raising an exhibitionist. I don't usually dress him that way, you know. He's in the school play tonight."

"So he told me." Connor was leaning against the front-door frame, arms crossed, insolently at ease. "The Little Prince." There was something biting in his tone.

"You sound as though you know it," she said.

"I do. In fact, I was in it when I was in third grade."

"That's funny. I thought only old-fashioned boys' schools like Stearns did plays like that any more."

Connor grinned. Clearly she couldn't imagine that a vagabond like himself would ever have gone to The Stearns School, or been on a friendly basis with the bank manager the way Jordan was now. *The transformation is complete*, he thought. *And it's damn well going to stay that way.*

If only Maggie Lewis didn't affect him this way! She passed close by him on her way out the door, and the nearness of her made him want to touch her again, to see those gold eyes open in languid passion the way they had after he'd kissed her last Friday night. And he couldn't, he thought. He just couldn't.

"Oh boy!" Jordan was shouting, as he caught sight of Connor's battle-scarred van parked behind Maggie's car. "I never rode in one of these before, Mom."

"And you're not going to now," Maggie returned. "Connor is a busy man, and I'm sure he doesn't want to be bothered ferrying us around. We'll take our car, and Connor can follow us in the van."

To her surprise, he answered pleasantly, "Who said I didn't want to be bothered?"

She frowned at him, wishing he'd stick to one mood at a time. His aggressiveness seemed to have disappeared, as though the fresh spring wind had blown it away. "If we go in separate cars, there's no need for you to come back here afterward," she pointed out. "You can go back to work, or wherever you're headed."

"Actually, I don't usually go to work until ten o'clock at night," he said. "I'm in no rush to get anywhere. And Jordan wants a ride in the van."

Maggie was amused at the thought of Jordan, in his fancy Edwardian costume, sitting in Connor's disreputable old van. "All right," she said, half against her better judgment. "It's not far, anyway."

Jordan was already in the van as she said the words, exclaiming over the racks of tools hanging inside. Connor held the door for Maggie, with a crooked grin on his face that made her wonder whether he was laughing at himself for being such a gentleman, or at her for her obvious reluctance to climb into the passenger seat. She couldn't help thinking of the last time she'd sat there, and she was pretty sure Connor knew it.

"Brings back memories, doesn't it?" he asked her. She wished he weren't quite so close and looking down into her face with that dark-eyed intensity.

"Yes," she replied, "and not very pleasant ones."

He raised an eyebrow. "Really?" he asked. "I seem to recall some very pleasant things about sitting next to you in this van."

The man had no right to stir her this way, Maggie thought. She could feel the pull of attraction between them, and resisting it only seemed to make it stronger. "The aftermath wasn't pleasant at all," she said firmly, amazed that a stranger's rejection should have the power to hurt her feelings after a week's breathing space. "Or do you find that most women enjoy being kissed and then told to get lost all in the same breath?"

He stopped grinning at that. "I'm sorry, Maggie," he said unexpectedly, and once again she wished he'd stick with one thing at a time. It was impossible to figure out what this man was up to. "There was a reason for my change of heart, believe it or not."

"Care to tell me what it was?"

He hesitated, glancing into the back as though hoping Jordan might provide him with a distraction. But the boy was contentedly looking over Connor's key-making equipment, and finally Connor turned back to meet Maggie's eyes. "Not now," he hedged.

She laughed, a little bitterly. "Well, time's running out," she said. "Once I hand you your eighty dollars, we have no more business together. And that suits me just fine."

Half an hour ago Connor had thought it would suit him just fine, too. Now he was wrapped up again in the spell of Maggie's golden eyes, and he knew he couldn't let things end here. "We'll see about that," he said, and forced a grin back onto his face. "Let's not keep your friendly bank manager waiting, Mrs. Lewis."

He put a hand on her elbow to help her up into the van, and Maggie marveled that he could manage to make such a simple gesture somehow sensual. Or maybe it was just her own response to him that made it seem that way.

She was glad Jordan was there. With her son on her lap and the seat belt around the two of them, she felt buffered from all the unaccountable things Connor made her feel. Things she hadn't felt for years, not since she'd fallen in love with Grant. A small, barely acknowledged whisper in her mind told her she hadn't felt these things even *with* Grant. No man had ever looked as deeply into her soul as Connor seemed to do.

"You work all night?" Jordan was saying, wonder in his voice.

"Sure do. From about ten till about seven in the morning."

"Wow. Mom only lets me stay up till ten o'clock about twice a year."

"I'm sure Connor didn't stay up all night when he was your age," Maggie said, and wondered why Connor's face seemed to cloud at her words.

Jordan was still marveling. "So when do you eat breakfast?" he wanted to know.

"When I get up—in the evening."

"You're up now," the boy pointed out.

"This is a special occasion. I got up extra early so I could come and see your mother before the banks closed," Connor replied.

"What's your bedtime, then?"

"Usually about noon."

The idea of going to bed at noon and eating breakfast in the evening obviously tickled Jordan's fancy. "So you eat dinner, let me see, in the morning, when you get home," he said.

"Yep. Around 8:00 a.m."

Jordan was giggling delightedly. "Then you go to bed at the same time I'm having my lunch," he exclaimed. "And you're just getting up when I'm going to bed!"

"That's about the size of it, kiddo." Connor seemed to be enjoying Jordan's enthusiasm, from the amused glance he shared with Maggie. "In the winter, sometimes I barely see the sun at all."

"Wow. Just like a vampire."

Connor threw back his head and laughed. "Maybe I should change my company name," he said. "What do you think about 'Dracula Locksmithing'?"

Maggie joined in their laughter, reserving judgment in that back corner of her mind. There *was* something uncanny about this night owl, for all his joking.

They were at a major intersection by now, and she was about to point out the right turn to Connor, but he turned the van that way without prompting, so she stayed silent. Just watching his strong, agile hands on the wheel was making her think of how they'd felt through her hair last week, and once again she was grateful for Jordan's irrepressible chatter.

"Hey, Mom," he was saying now. "When I grow up, I'm going to work all night like Connor. Then when we go to Grandma's for Sunday dinner, it'll be like eating at midnight!"

"Are you sure you'd like to eat roast beef and potatoes at midnight?" Maggie asked him gravely.

"Sure, because then I could wear my pajamas to the table and not have to put on my jacket and tie." Jordan giggled again.

The shadow on Connor's handsome face was more pronounced this time, and Maggie wondered what was causing it. Was he such a free spirit that he couldn't stand the thought of a small boy cooped up in a suit?

"Dinner at my mother-in-law's is a family ritual," she said, wondering if he'd explain the black look he was favoring the windshield with. "And rather formal. It sometimes strikes me as a little silly—just the three of us at this table the size of a shuffleboard court—but it means a lot to Jordan's grandmother."

"My grandfather died last year," Jordan chimed in. "He was a great guy."

I know, Connor wanted to say. *He was my father's best friend, the way your father was my best friend*. He could feel himself being drawn back into the circle he'd left so emphatically, and for the life of him he couldn't decide whether he wanted to fight it or not.

"Anyway," Jordan went on, oblivious to the undercurrents in the front seat of the van, "when I grow up, I can stay up all night if I want to, just like you. Right, Connor?"

"Right, kiddo."

The two of them nodded at each other and Maggie felt somehow left out, excluded from Jordan's innocence and Connor's appealing bohemianism. She envied them both, suddenly and fiercely, and resented this good-looking rogue who'd dropped into her life without warning and made such a major upheaval over a measly eighty bucks.

She stayed silent, fighting inwardly against the familiar trapped feeling that still overwhelmed her now and again, until the van pulled smoothly into the parking lot of her bank. Then she sat bolt upright, released Jordan from the seat belt and turned slowly to look at Connor.

Connor undid his own seat belt, slowly becoming aware that something was wrong with Maggie. Her eyes were troubled when he met their gaze.

"What's the matter?" he asked casually. "I got you here in one piece, didn't I?"

"Yes," she admitted, "but how on earth did you know where 'here' is?"

Connor started to laugh, and then her meaning sunk in. For a moment he just sat and stared blankly at her, amazed at what he'd done.

Of course, he'd driven to this bank. The Lewises and the Blakes had banked here for over a hundred years. His own third cousin was an investment counselor here. He didn't know the current manager, but he'd been on a first-name basis with his predecessor fifteen years ago. There was a trust fund with Connor's name on it at this very branch, although he hadn't touched a penny of the money since he'd turned twenty-two.

He'd driven here without thinking, and now he was going to have to think pretty fast to make up for the lapse.

"Funny thing," he said, with a laugh that didn't sound too convincing to his own ears. "This is the only bank I know in Wellesley. I used to do business here. I guess I just drove here automatically. Quite a coincidence, huh?"

"Quite a coincidence," Maggie echoed. Connor couldn't tell if she believed a word of it, and when she asked him if he'd like to come in with them, he suspected it was some sort of a test.

"No, thanks," he said hastily. "I'll wait out here."

She was still watching him far too closely as she left the van.

With a groan, Connor settled back in the driver's seat and watched her shepherding her son through the bank's front door. He should make a break for it now, he told himself. Just start the engine and go. He'd let her keep the eighty bucks—not that Grant Lewis's widow would ever have to count her pennies—and consider the whole thing as a learning experience.

If he stayed, sooner or later he was going to have to tell her who he was. And then there would be no way to avoid getting involved in the family business again, as his father had been insisting he do for the past four years.

Connor groaned again, and crossed his arms tightly. He could feel the frustration bunching up in his muscles, and knew that there wasn't a way in the world he could have Maggie Lewis without having everything that went along with her—the traditions, the business, the Sunday dinners in suits and ties.

And yet the tension in him was because of her, because of the way he wanted to reach out and hold her close to him. *Damn!* he thought angrily. He'd been the black sheep too long to go willingly back into the fold now.

The ride back to Maggie's house was quiet. Even Jordan seemed to sense the strain in the air. When they pulled into the driveway, Maggie carefully counted out eighty dollars in cash and handed it over to Connor. He just as carefully wrote out a receipt and gave it to her.

"Nice doing business with you, Mrs. Lewis," he said. She couldn't imagine what that note was in his deep voice. It almost sounded like regret, but that made no sense at all.

"And with you, Connor Whatever-Your-Name-Is." She smiled as she handed her keys to Jordan and watched him dash to the front door. "Now he'll go back to being an aspiring actor, and forget all about wanting to be an all-night locksmith," she said, turning back to Connor.

"What about you?" His voice was slightly husky. "Will you forget all about me, too?"

Her smile lingered in her eyes, and it was all Connor could do to keep from taking her in his arms as he had before. "No," she said thoughtfully, "I don't think I will."

"Good." His voice was tight.

"I must go," she said, reaching for the door handle. "I have to get some food into both of us before the play."

"Maggie, wait."

She turned back to him almost eagerly, as though expecting—what? What could he say to prolong this moment?

"I...want you to know that I don't usually kiss women I've just met. And I don't make a habit of running out on them immediately afterward."

He loved the honest, assessing look in her eyes. It seemed to let him straight into her thoughts. "Why did you do those things with me, then?" she asked him.

"I kissed you because I found you so attractive that I couldn't do anything else," he said simply and truthfully. The next part was trickier. "And I backed off because, well, I was startled that things happened so fast, that's all. I guess I just got carried away by the moment."

"I know what you mean," she said softly. "And I find you very attractive, too." She paused, looking so intently at him that he could feel the desire welling up inside. He knew the welcoming warmth of her lips, and his mind was swimming with images of more.

"Maybe you could call me sometime," she said, lifting his spirits to giddy heights. And then she let them down again by adding impishly, "When you're ready to tell me who you really are, I mean."

"Persistent, aren't you?"

"So my husband always used to tell me."

Now, why had she thrown that in? To discourage him, by bringing up the memory of her husband? Connor decided to explore a little further.

"Did your husband die suddenly?" he asked, although he already knew.

"Yes. It was a blood clot in his brain. It happened overnight."

"Must have been a hell of a shock."

"It was." She almost smiled, and a rueful look came into her eyes. "It took two or three years before I stopped expecting to see him in all the old places. You know, listening for him to drive up every day at five-thirty."

"Sounds like he kept a pretty regular schedule."

"Oh, he did. He was a very traditional man, in a lot of ways."

"I guess that appeals to you, huh?"

Once again, Maggie wondered why he was probing her so deeply. There must be something behind it; the way he was scuffing his boot-clad heel in the gravel of her driveway seemed too elaborately casual.

Part of her wanted to tell him the whole story. The rest of her said *Wait until he's given you some answers.* All of her was pleased at the thought that this relationship, unlikely though it was, might possibly go somewhere.

She realized he was still waiting for an answer. "My childhood was nontraditional in all the wrong ways," she said guardedly, "so I guess I have good reason to find this kind of life appealing." She waved a hand broadly at her neatly kept house and lawn. "I really have to go, Connor. Call me if you ever feel like telling me any of *your* secrets."

And then she was gone, before he could give in to the crazy impulse to astonish her by saying *I'm Kincaid Connor Blake. What do you think of that?*

Just as well, he thought glumly as he shifted the van into reverse and tore out of the quiet neighborhood with a most un-Wellesley-like screech of tires. She couldn't have picked a better way to hold him at arm's length if she'd tried.

Somewhere in the darkness a telephone was ringing. Maggie rolled over in her bed and fumbled for the light, still half asleep. She had a foggy recollection that she was late for something—was Jordan supposed to be at school for the play?—and then she remembered that the play was over. She squinted at her bedside clock.

She wasn't supposed to be anywhere, except asleep. It was two in the morning, and her voice was brusque as she answered the phone.

"How about dinner together on Sunday?" a familiar voice demanded.

Maggie propped herself up on one elbow and smothered a curse. Just because the man worked such crazy hours didn't give him the right to wake her up in the middle of the night. "Who is this, please?" she asked sweetly.

"You know perfectly well who it is, Maggie. Did I wake you up?"

"Of course, you woke me up. There are still people who sleep at night, you know."

"I'd almost forgotten." She could picture that tilted grin, and knew it was a mistake to have conjured up his image. It made his deep, warm voice too hard to resist. "And I'm sorry I woke you. It was...an impulse. I knew if I didn't call you right now, I wouldn't do it."

"I have to go to Sunday dinner at my mother-in-law's," she said, answering his original question.

"I know you do. How about after that? Leave Jordan with her and come for a drive with me."

"A drive to where?"

"Hard to say. You never know, when you get in the van with me, where you're going to end up."

You certainly don't, she thought. He'd taken her to some surprising places already. "Does this mean you're ready to break down and tell me the deep, dark secret of your last name?" she asked.

There was a pause, as if he were wrestling with the impulse that had made him call. "No, it doesn't," he said finally, and with finality. "If you come with me, it has to be because you want to see me, with or without a last name."

What on earth was the man hiding? Maggie couldn't guess. But one thing, at least, was abundantly clear. "I do want to see you," she acknowledged. Would she have been so honest if he'd called her at 2:00 p.m. instead of a.m., she wondered? Probably not, and the son of a gun probably knew that.

"Good. I'll pick you up at your place at two, then. And I should warn you: Sunday with me is a little on the informal side."

"Why doesn't that surprise me?" She found herself laughing as she hung up the phone. Clearly Connor was the stuff dreams are made of, she thought. There was something about him that went perfectly with the upside-down logic of the dreamworld he'd wakened her from.

Three

Blaa-a-a-t!

The van's horn broke through the afternoon stillness, and made Maggie jump as she grabbed her jacket from the hall cupboard. She was out the door and halfway down the driveway by the time the noise had finished reverberating around her quiet neighborhood.

"You know, you could have walked up and rung the doorbell," she said, as Connor appeared at the side of the van to open the passenger door for her. "That horn sounds like it belongs on a Mack truck."

There it was, that independent grin she'd had such a hard time getting out of her head. "I was going to ring the doorbell," he said, "but you didn't give me a chance. Anyway, I like to announce my presence, as you may have noticed."

"I have noticed," she said pointedly. "The first time we met, you soaked me to the skin announcing your presence. And now you do it by disturbing all my neighbors."

"Ah, the neighbors." He was still smiling as he climbed into the driver's seat and started the van. "I'd forgotten what it was like to worry about what the neighbors are thinking."

Maggie didn't like what he was implying. "It's just that the old man in the next house always has a nap on Sunday afternoons," she said. "And the people across the street are constantly on my case about the day-care center..." She let her words trail off, realizing how ultrarespectable she must seem to Connor. "I suppose you don't have neighbors to worry about, wherever you live," she added.

She was trying to find out more about him, but he neatly sidestepped the question. "Oh, I have them, all right," he said. "I just don't worry about them."

"Sometimes I think that must be nice," Maggie sighed, settling into the bucket seat and pushing her hands into her coat pockets.

"I thought you said your nice, respectable life appealed to you," he said.

She shot a quick glance over at him. "Parts of it do," she admitted, "but there are parts I could do without." She didn't want him to ask her which parts she meant, so she added quickly, "I don't suppose you ever get tired of *your* life-style. Being awake when everyone else is asleep, I mean."

Up until last week that life-style had suited him perfectly. But now he was having serious problems with it, and all because of the woman sitting next to him. He tried fiercely to concentrate on his driving, but his eyes were constantly distracted by the slight kissable pout of her full lower lip. Suddenly its seductive charm seemed so much more worthwhile than the career he'd made for himself.

"Sometimes I get tired of it," he said curtly, and steered hard to the right onto an entrance ramp.

Maggie looked at him again, but let his answer stand. "Where are we going, anyway?" she asked him.

Connor was merging with the northbound traffic on Route 128, the highway that ringed Metropolitan Boston. "Wait and see," he said. He drove without speaking for a while, and then commented, "I'm glad to see you decided I meant what I said about dressing informally."

She glanced down at her jeans and the heavy beige fisherman's knit sweater she'd had for years. Her dark brown corduroy jacket was also a favorite from before she'd married Grant. Somehow, these old faithfuls had seemed appropriate to her mystery outing with Connor.

"It's funny," she said. "I actually felt a little guilty changing out of my good dress and into comfortable clothes. Sunday afternoons are such an institution for us. This is a little like playing hooky."

How well Connor remembered that feeling! He'd always seized every opportunity to shed his hated tie and jacket and grub around in the woods behind his parents' house. "Sounds pretty stuffy," he said. "How does Jordan feel about it?"

"Oh, I don't think he minds, really. It's always a special occasion for him, and his grandmother indulges him far more than I ever do."

"She didn't mind baby-sitting him this afternoon, then?"

"No. She's been very lonely since her husband died, and she's thrilled to have Jordan around. He's been teaching her to play video games," she added with a smile. The image of stately Caroline Lewis, sitting in front of the screen with her perfectly coiffed white hair and elegant linen dress, still tickled her.

To her surprise, Connor didn't share in her smile. She wondered what he was thinking, as he gazed fiercely out at the traffic. She couldn't figure him out, at all.

He asked her about the neutral subject of her day-care center, and she described how she'd felt the need to do something new after her husband died. "We'd always envisioned a big family," she said. "That was what the playroom was for, anyway, so it seemed logical to fill the place up with kids, even if they were other people's.''

"But you don't—'' What was the least awkward way to phrase it? "The day-care center isn't something you need to do for the income, is it?''

She looked levelly at him. "You're a very nosy man,'' she informed him.

"One of my many bad habits.'' Her comment didn't seem to bother him. "It's just that, well, it's common knowledge that the Lewises are a wealthy family. Presumably you don't have to work if you don't want to.''

Maggie was silent for so long that he wondered if he'd really put his foot in it with his bluntness. Finally she said, a little coldly, "Maybe you shouldn't put too much stock in common knowledge.'' Her eyes had that glitter that told him she was guarding some feeling that ran very deeply indeed.

He held up a placating hand. "I didn't mean to pry,'' he assured her. "I wondered, that's all.'' She'd bristled like a briar hedge when he'd gotten too personal, and so he kept the conversation to safer subjects as he steered the van north, then east, toward the ocean. He'd get back to the mystery that was Maggie Lewis soon enough.

The day was warm and windy, and Maggie's mood was as restless as the breeze stirring the trees beside the highway. Something about being with Connor stirred so many half-forgotten longings in her, feelings from a time before she'd married and joined the genteel world of the Lewis family. She had too many obligations now to be as free and easy as Connor obviously was, but just for this afternoon, she was letting herself revel in the breath of fresh air he seemed to bring to her life.

"Now I know where we're going,'' she said, as Connor turned the wheel. "This is Marblehead, isn't it?''

"Good guess.'' Connor steered the van down the increasingly narrow road that led to the center of the old harbor town.

"It wasn't a guess. My husband used to keep his yacht here, not that he ever had much time to use it. But several weekends every summer we would come up and go sailing."

"Do you like to sail?"

Maggie's face lit up. "Oh, yes," she said. "It's so wonderful. You point the bow out to the open sea and you feel as though you could go anywhere in the world. Have you ever gone?"

"Me? I've gone sailing a few times." More like a few hundred, Connor thought, remembering the hours he and Grant had spent together on the water as boys. "Of course, you need to be rich to indulge in a sport like that." He watched her face carefully.

"I suppose," she said, a trifle defensively.

"Do you still have your husband's boat?"

"No. I was never a good enough sailor to handle it by myself, and there wasn't anyone else who wanted to sail with me."

"That's too bad."

"It was. I miss it." She glanced at him, as if she wanted to say more but wasn't sure she should. Then she made up her mind. "My mother-in-law gets seasick just standing on the pier, and Grant's sister, Bobbie, isn't much better. My father-in-law loved to sail, but he was already ailing by the time Grant died. It didn't seem right to keep the boat and never use it."

"Lots of people do," he commented. They'd reached the waterfront by now and Connor nodded at the crowded harbor, filled with sailboats bobbing in the waves. "For some folks, having a yacht is just something they do. It's a status symbol, I guess. They don't care whether the boat gets used much or not."

"I know some people like that." Her tone said clearly that she might know them, but she didn't have to like them. "You seem to have a chip on your shoulder about rich people, Connor. Does money make you uncomfortable?"

"No, but the life-style that goes with it does," he said bluntly.

"That's rather a sweeping statement."

"It comes from experience, believe me," he returned. "And I'm not talking about every rich person on the planet. The life-style that bothers me is a very specific one."

"Let me guess. You're talking about old New England money, aren't you?" She thought of the aggressive way he'd behaved in her quiet Wellesley home, as though he felt compelled to make a statement against the understated wealth he saw there.

"Bingo. People who buy yachts and never use them. People who think every generation is going to be just the same as the last. People who have fancy summer places on Marblehead Neck."

"If I'm not mistaken, that's where we're heading right now."

"Just because I don't like their style, does that mean I can't enjoy their view of the ocean?" he demanded. His voice was overly casual again, and Maggie sensed him trying to back off from the strong stance he'd just taken. There was definitely something personal in his remarks about rich New England families, she thought.

Maybe he'd been cheated by someone in the past, and that explained his sour attitude. It was possible; Maggie knew lots of wealthy people who could be as stingy as Scrooge. That would explain his anger on Friday over her bounced check, and his refusal to take a customer's word for anything.

She looked more closely at him. He was whistling and seemingly carefree, with his thick, black hair tousled and shading his forehead. His changes of mood were so sudden that she couldn't hope to keep up with them or understand what they meant. She'd been enjoying the sense of freedom his company gave her, but now she reminded herself that sometimes freedom wasn't a good thing. Sometimes it was better to be safe, as she'd been taught half her lifetime ago.

"There's a nice park at the end of the Neck," she ventured, because the silence in the van was starting to feel uncomfortable to her.

"I know, but that's not where we're going. I hope you didn't eat too much Sunday dinner, because I haven't eaten since this morning and I'm getting pretty hungry."

She hadn't seen any signs of food when she'd gotten into the van, but she passed up the obvious question of where they were going to eat and concentrated instead on Connor's crazy schedule. "Let's see," she said. "Dinner for you is early in the morning, when you get home, right?"

"Right."

"Didn't you sleep today?"

"I caught a few hours' sleep. I don't need much. But my stomach thinks it's time for something, since I'm awake."

She had to smile. "So do we get bacon and eggs?"

"Give me credit for a bit more class than that," he replied. His deep voice was teasing. "You'll see before long."

They were following the road that circled Marblehead Neck, and Maggie could see glimpses of the enormous summer homes that faced the ocean on one side of the small peninsula and the harbor on the other. She hoped they were going to the ocean side; it had been too long since she'd seen that expanse of salt water.

She was in luck. Before long Connor halted the van in front of an imposing wrought-iron gate, and hopped down from the driver's seat. Through the bare branches of the surrounding trees, Maggie saw a gray stone house, with honest-to-goodness turrets on each of its four corners. And past the house, she could see the slate gray of the sea. The familiar salty tang was a welcome reminder of the hours she'd spent sailing with Grant, but even the nearness of the ocean couldn't take the edge off her curiosity about what Connor was doing.

He'd pulled a bunch of keys from his pocket and was calmly unlocking the gate as though it was his personal property. Maggie frowned as she watched. She half expected a guard dog to charge them or an alarm to go off, but the place remained quiet and undisturbed even after Connor had driven the van through the gate and locked it behind them.

"Now, wait a minute," Maggie said, turning to face him in her seat. "How does an itinerant locksmith like you get the key to a private estate like this one?"

"Getting keys is the easiest thing in the world—for a locksmith," he replied glibly, and her frown deepened. Was he really implying that he'd gotten the key by some underhanded means? Or was he just toying with her? He was fully capable of doing either one, she knew by now.

"Connor, before we go any farther, I'd like some reassurance that we're not breaking and entering, all right?" She wished she didn't sound so prim, but she just couldn't help feeling nervous.

His grin seemed to taunt her. "What's the matter?" he asked. She could see the sparkle in his nearly black eyes, and she wished she knew what the hell it meant. "Don't you trust me?"

"Of course I don't trust you." Her prompt answer knocked his grin back a notch or two, she was glad to see. "Why should I trust a man who won't even tell me his last name? Whose place is this, anyway?" There had been a discreet brass plate on the gate, but Maggie hadn't been able to read the name on it.

"Someone who doesn't mind that we're using it," he replied, grudgingly.

"I'd feel better if you'd tell me the name of the owner."

"Sorry, I can't do that." Connor climbed back into the van, wanting to get safely past the gate so that Maggie couldn't see Miss Lucella Blake's name on the plaque, and jump to her own conclusions. "But if it makes you feel a little less criminal, I *will* tell you that the owner is an elderly lady who'd been having a lot of problems with vandalism. She only lives here in the summer, you see."

"I see." Maggie knew that many of the mansions here, like the sailboats in the harbor, were unused for much of the year.

"Anyway, she hired me to make the place burglarproof. And I did, and as part payment she lets me use the grounds whenever I have an urge to come to the shore."

"I didn't realize you did burglarproofing, too."

He grinned at her. "It's sort of a sideline," he said, "but I do have a yet-to-be patented system that I'd bet on against any thief I've ever encountered."

"You should market it, if it's that good."

"Maybe someday I will. You need investment funds for that, and marketing skills and a lot of other stuff I'm not interested in." His explanations had suddenly gotten very brusque, she noted. "So, does that reassure you?" he demanded finally.

"I suppose so. It's just that—"

"It's just that someone with your background can't imagine doing anything on the wrong side of the law, is that it?"

There it was again, that blatant assumption that she was a wholehearted part of the oak-paneled world she inhabited now. "That's the worst kind of reverse snobbism," she informed him hotly, feeling her temper start to rise. *Three meetings, three displays of temper*, she thought in amazement. Whoever Connor really was, he certainly knew how to get under her skin.

"Snobbism!" He seemed stung by the word.

"Absolutely. You automatically assume it's bad to have money. That's just as snobbish as assuming it's bad *not* to have money."

And here he'd left the bosom of his family to avoid being labeled a snob, Connor thought. He didn't like what Maggie was saying, or the possibility that she might be right. He hit back before she could say anything else.

"It must be nice to lead such a sheltered life that you can't even imagine doing anything illegal," he said, more to see her reaction than anything else.

It was gratifyingly quick. "As it happens, you're dead wrong about that," she said.

"What did you do, cheat on your final exams at finishing school?"

Maggie clenched her teeth and tried to stay calm. But the man really was asking for it, and she let fly with the truth without stopping to think that she'd never even told Grant about this particular episode of her life.

"Nothing quite that tame," she said. "No finishing school would have taken me even if I'd wanted to go. No, I stole some jewelry from a rich woman. Is that exciting enough for you?"

She saw his eyes widen in surprise and congratulated herself. "Why did you do that?" he wanted to know, sounding genuinely interested.

She shrugged, not sure how far into this she wanted to go. "I needed the money or thought I did," she said. "And I was just a kid, with a lot of friends who never thought twice about stealing things."

"Peer pressure can be tough," he said, speculatively.

"It was. I might have gone on from there, if a woman I admired very much hadn't talked some sense into me."

"Your mother, I suppose." Something in the fondness of her tone made Connor guess that.

"No, it was actually the woman I stole the jewelry from." She paused, and decided to let loose one more revelation. "My mother was her maid."

He eyed her thoughtfully. "I guess you really *did* grow up on the other side of the tracks, didn't you?" he said.

"Actually, by that time I was living in a big house in Westchester County, but only because my mother's job was live-in. Up to that point we'd been living in a part of Newark, New Jersey that probably won't ever make *House Beautiful*. And until Mrs. Corviser took me in hand, my manners were much more Newark than Westchester County." She smiled, remembering the tough, angry teen-ager she'd been.

"Cinderella's fairy godmother," Connor speculated.

"Something like that," she admitted. Then she decided that that was enough skeletons from the closet for now, and she went on hastily, "I really didn't eat much lunch, now that I come to think of it, and I'm getting hungry, too. When did you say breakfast was?"

He waited a long moment before replying, and then seemed to let her get away with her obvious change of subject. The penetrating interest in his dark eyes was still there, though, and she had a feeling her disclosures might come back to haunt her.

"Breakfast should be ready any time now," he said, looking at his wrist. His watch, like his van and the brown leather jacket he was wearing again today, showed the scars of many years of hard use. Like his face, she thought. Like the strong hand that was reaching in her direction. For an instant she thought he was reaching for her, and felt the now-familiar tug of anticipation.

But he stopped just short of her knee, and instead tugged at the clasp that held the metal cover over the part of the van's engine that was actually inside the vehicle, between the two seats. Another tug released the clasps on Connor's side. Then he lifted the cover, and Maggie was confronted with a row of neatly wrapped foil packages, sitting on the warm engine and smelling, when he opened them, like a combination French restaurant and gasoline station.

"What on earth?" was as far as she got before he grinned at her.

"Yep," he said, enjoying her puzzled look. "Nearly done. Let's just find a more scenic spot than the driveway, and we can eat."

Maggie was silent as he pulled the van down the curving driveway and onto a deeply rutted dirt road that led through a grove of trees and stopped just short of a stone seawall.

Ahead of them was the whole Atlantic, bordered by Marblehead Neck's rocky coast and dotted by colored buoy markers and the odd brave spring sailor.

For a moment Maggie lost herself in the allure of the ocean, traveling in spirit with the crew of the nearest yacht she could see. Its white sails were taut in the strong wind, and the spray looked cold and exhilarating. She caught her breath with the longing that the smell of the sea always called up in her. She remembered trying to explain that longing to Grant, who hadn't understood. Why did she have the sense that Connor would know instinctively what she was feeling?

Something in his silence made her doubly certain. When he finally spoke, his voice held none of its usual mocking tone. "It's something you never get complacent about, isn't it?" he asked.

"Yes." She turned to him almost shyly, as though he'd managed to discover another one of her secrets. "It's like another fresh start, every time you look at it."

They were both silent for another long minute, and Maggie somehow wasn't surprised when Connor reached over the warm engine hood and took her hand. It was like that moment when he'd kissed her, all over again. The two of them had the power to set the whole world aside, just for an instant, and share something rare and powerful.

She tightened her hand around his, and felt his pulse in her fingertips. When she raised her eyes to meet his, she was almost shocked by the potent need in his face. Whatever else he was hiding from her, this was real and honest. Surely no man could look at a woman like that unless she stirred him to his very bones.

She looked away quickly, not daring to let herself respond to that charged look. And yet she knew she was already too late; her heartbeat was pounding in answer to the hunger in his eyes, and the unsteady pulsing deep inside her told her that her mysterious locksmith had already managed to unlock more than one door without waiting to be invited.

She wasn't nearly ready to let her feelings run away with her, and she took refuge in a smaller mystery with a feeling of relief. "All right, Connor, let's get to the hard questions," she said, forcing a flippancy she didn't quite feel. "What's under the engine cover?"

His grin was as shaky as her words, but he seemed to be making the same effort to sound calm. "Breakfast," he said simply. "Or dinner, as you daytime types would call it."

"You keep it warm on the engine?"

"No, I cook it on the engine." Once again he undid the clasps of the engine cover, and this time he took the four rectangular packs out. "Ow!" he said, shaking his fingers. "I don't know why I can never remember to bring a pot holder along."

Maggie was laughing by now, the awkwardness of a moment ago receding. "I don't believe it," she said. "Do you cook all your meals this way?"

"All the ones I eat on the road. I usually wrap something up and slap it on the engine block when I go to work, and by the time I've made five or six calls, my lunch is ready."

He pulled two plates and forks from a compartment behind his seat, and set them on the engine cover. "This way, I even get to warm the plates," he grinned. "Just like the fancy restaurants do."

"What are we having?" Maggie was frankly curious as he unwrapped the foil.

"Veal scaloppine stuffed with spinach and Fontina cheese," he announced. "And on the side, green beans with almonds. Would madam care for anything to drink?"

"Madam is so overwhelmed that she's going to leave the rest of the decisions up to you." Maggie wasn't at all surprised to see him produce a bottle of white wine from somewhere in the back of the van, and put a practiced hand on its side to test the temperature.

"Just right," he announced. "That's one advantage to these older vans—plenty of cold spots for chilling things."

She gave him a delighted smile. "The van as kitchen," she marveled, shaking her head. "I never would have thought of it. When did you discover this talent for cooking on the road?"

He was opening the wine, his fingers dexterously twisting the corkscrew. "It started one night when I knew there wasn't going to be time to grab a bite," he said. "I had some leftover lasagna wrapped in foil, so I brought it along. Throwing it on the engine block to warm it up was an inspiration, and it worked so well I decided to experiment with cooking things from scratch. It would take a week of hard driving to cook a pot roast," he confessed, "but things like chicken breasts and veal cutlets work like a charm."

"You're a very surprising man, Connor," she told him gravely, but with dancing eyes.

He managed to fight down the excitement that her glittering look always stirred up, and accepted her words as a compliment. "You ain't seen nothin' yet," he muttered. The more time he spent with her, the less he knew how to deal with the inevitable problem of telling her who he really was. His thoughts kept turning to the current state of affairs for the Lewises and Blakes, and the future of the investment firm that bound the two families so closely together.

After he'd served Maggie's dinner and his own, and filled two wineglasses with the good French Chablis he'd been saving for a special occasion, he turned to her and said offhandedly, "Tell me more about your husband." She excited so much more than just his curiosity, and it was time to start finding out more about her.

She looked surprised at his words. "You mean, what was he like?" she asked him.

Connor already knew what Grant had been like. He was more interested in Maggie, now. "I mean, why did you marry him?" he said. "You must have been very young when you got married. Was he older than you?'' He picked his words carefully, not wanting to give himself away.

"Yes, twelve years older. I was twenty when we got married, and he was thirty-two.''

She seemed reluctant to go on, and Connor prompted her, "How did you meet?''

"I was working for an interior-decorating firm that was redoing his office. He worked for his family's firm. It's called International Investments, Incorporated, or Triple I to the family. Anyway, they've always been a sort of stodgy, old Boston firm, but Grant had new ideas about sprucing up their image, beginning with the office.''

She smiled, as though the memories she was reliving were pleasant ones, and Connor felt an involuntary clenching of the muscles in his stomach. He'd never felt jealous of Grant in their years growing up together but, by God, he did now. The thought of Maggie with any other man was surprisingly painful.

"I was a very junior decorator,'' Maggie went on, "so I did a lot of the legwork, and Grant and I saw a lot of each other. He said I looked so appealing, peering at him from around the potted palms I was installing, that he couldn't help falling in love.''

Grant *would* say something like that, Connor thought. Predictable and safe, that was Grant's way. Connor himself would have been more likely to swing down from the potted palm and carry Maggie off to a desert island somewhere. But maybe that wasn't what she'd wanted. Maybe she preferred the safety Grant had offered.

"We were married for only three years,'' she was saying, and her voice was steady although she refused to meet his eyes. "Jordan was only two when his father died. He barely remembers Grant. If I hadn't had to keep myself together for Jordan's sake—'' She shook her head suddenly, as if clearing the unhappy memories from it. "This veal is wonderful, by the way. I'd ask you for the recipe, but I'm not sure I do enough driving to be able to duplicate it.''

All right, Connor thought. *Change the subject again. We'll get back to it sooner or later.*

They chatted for an hour about other things, mostly Connor's adventures in the years before he'd decided on a more or less settled career as a locksmith. He told her about his cross-country treks, and how he'd worked his way from coast to coast several times, taking jobs doing everything from building houses to roping steers.

"I thought there was a little bit of cowboy in you," she teased.

"More than a little bit, ma'am," he assured her.

Some of his yarns strained the imagination. Did anyone really tackle survivalist camping alone for six months in the wilderness with no tools but a knife and an old hatchet? But something in his manner told her that all his stories were true, and it made her ache again for the adventures she'd never had and for the experience that was etched in the strong, humorous lines of Connor's face. His fierce will had led him to do these things, she could tell, and his sense of humor had enabled him to survive.

At some point Maggie became aware that the sun was sinking, and the ocean view in front of them looked colder and bleaker than it had. All the sailboats had headed for the harbor, and after a glance at her watch, she suggested to Connor that it was time for them to do the same thing.

"I told my mother-in-law I'd pick Jordan up before seven," she said. "She has a committee meeting to go to this evening, and I don't want to hold her up."

"Well, we certainly don't want to keep the committee waiting," Connor said, and Maggie was startled by the sarcasm in his tone. He started to turn the key in the ignition, and then paused.

He was constantly amazed at the conflicts this woman stirred up in him. On the one hand, she brought back so many old associations that he'd gratefully escaped from—Sunday dinners, the conservative Triple I office building, the

endless committee meetings, the sense of duty that had stifled Connor for half his life.

And on the other hand...

He sighed, and put the key back in his pocket. "Indulge
me just for another five minutes," he said. "I never feel like
I've really seen the ocean until I've walked on the shore and
had my hair all messed up by the wind." Her sudden smile,
as she flung open her door and joined him on the wide lawn
of the summer estate, told him she'd been longing for that
herself.

The wind was colder than he'd expected, and he put an
arm around Maggie's shoulders as they walked down to the
rocky shore. He felt ridiculously warm inside when he felt
her put her arm around his waist in response.

"Whose place is this, Connor?" she was asking, above
the noise of the sea breeze. "Why the big secret?"

"I've always thought life would be boring without a few
secrets," he said, not giving anything away.

"Somehow I have the feeling life is never boring around
you," she returned. "Were you always such a law unto
yourself?"

He stopped, balancing their combined weight on a
boulder scarred by a thousand years of waves. "Yes," he
said, turning her to face him. "Right from the beginning.
Does that bother you?" It seemed important to know.

"No," she said, and he had to catch the word quickly
before the wind tore it out to sea. "No, it doesn't bother me.
It...excites me."

"Good." His voice was rough with the passion he'd been
reining in all afternoon, with the need to touch her that was
constant and pressing whenever she turned those bewitching gold-and-hazel eyes on him.

The waves crashing on the rocks around them were like an
echo of what he was feeling inside. He lowered his head and
tasted her lips, first gently, and then with a hunger he
couldn't control and didn't even want to. He knew she
wanted this, too, knew it from the immediate response of

her soft lips and the wordless moan that he could barely hear over the noise of the sea. Her need fueled his, and threatened to sweep them both away.

Maggie wrapped both arms around Connor's waist and held on as if her life depended on it. His mouth was moving over hers with a certainty that stirred dangerous feelings deep inside her. She parted her teeth and felt his tongue twine with hers in a sweet, mindless embrace. Her last rational thoughts evaporated then, and she let herself go willingly into this new realm of desire and sensation that seemed half made of Connor and half of the pounding sea around them.

His fingers were feathering through her hair, following the tracks of the wind. Maggie closed her eyes and let the salty air and Connor's enticing male scent mingle in her senses. She knew this was only for the moment, but for the moment she didn't care who he was or why he stirred her like this.

His lips were exploring her skin now, finding hidden places that had never received such sweet attention—the hollow of her temple, the softness of her earlobe, the base of her neck. Every part of her that he kissed was humming with desire. When he ran a knowing hand over the bulk of her sweater and the roundness of her breasts, she gave a sudden cry of need.

She sought his lips again, as though kissing him could satisfy the hunger she felt. It couldn't, of course. The instant his mouth met hers, she was swept up to a new height, a greater need, until her imagination took her inexorably ahead to thoughts of making love with Connor, losing herself in the strength of his passion and the release she knew he could bring her.

"Connor," she murmured, and felt him tighten his hold on her slender frame. Then he raised his head, and although she'd told herself already that nothing this man did would surprise her, she *was* surprised to hear him laugh.

"Don't look now," he said huskily, "but we're about to be stranded on a desert island."

She opened her eyes slowly, and saw that the waves were lapping around the base of the boulder they were standing on. "The tide must be coming in," she said.

"Yes, and it's in a hurry, too, from the looks of things. Or maybe we've been standing here for hours. It wouldn't surprise me." His dark eyes were grave as he reached up a hand to trace the outline of her face, and she wished she had some idea of what was going on in that mind of his.

"Come on," he said briskly, as though he saw her curiosity and wanted to avoid it. "If we jump now, we'll get off with nothing more than a few damp toes."

Maggie's toes were a little more than damp by the time they'd made their way back to the staircase in the stone seawall, but she barely noticed the discomfort. Her body was still reacting to Connor's nearness and the troublesome images his kiss had conjured up. She craved his sense of freedom, his devil-may-care attitude, even as she told herself firmly that a single mother with a business to run and an inheritance to manage couldn't take the world quite as casually as the good-looking gypsy beside her.

Connor took good care, once again, that Maggie couldn't glimpse the name of Blake on the wrought-iron gate as they left the estate. He had a feeling she was very attracted to his vagabond image, and he didn't want to take a chance yet on her finding out he was really just the boy next door.

Four

Connor was trying—honestly trying—to remember the last time he'd worn a jacket and tie. His sister Jacquie's wedding, he supposed, a good ten years ago. He doubted he'd had his charcoal gray tweed or his one tie, a rich burgundy red silk, off the hanger since then.

His throat felt constricted as he pulled the knot tighter. What was he getting himself into here, he wondered?

He'd found himself uncharacteristically at a loss for words after his encounter on the shore with Maggie last week. The depth of what he'd felt then had shaken him up, and made him take a hard look at just where he was heading. He'd carefully avoided making plans to see her again, figuring he'd better sort out his own feelings first, but when she'd called him on Wednesday and invited him to come to Sunday dinner, he'd said yes without a second thought.

And look where it had landed him, he thought almost glumly, staring at his reflection in the full-length mirror next to his bed in the corner of his big loft that he used as a bedroom. Roped into a jacket and tie for Sunday dinner after all these years, just because he didn't seem to be able to resist the golden sparkle in a woman's eyes.

"Is your mother-in-law going to be there?" he'd thought to ask her, remembering just in time that Caroline Lewis would know him immediately as the black sheep of the Blake family.

"No. She's going out of town to visit friends. That's why Jordan and I are on our own."

Well, at least he and Jordan could commiserate about having their windpipes choked because of some ridiculously outmoded convention of male fashion, he thought. He felt like a stranger to himself as he drove from South Boston to Wellesley, and by the time he climbed Maggie's doorstep and rang the doorbell, he was almost having second thoughts. He heard the quiet chime inside the house. Nothing noisy, he reflected; everything correct and polite. Then he heard small, echoing footsteps in the foyer that weren't polite at all. Jordan threw open the door with enthusiasm, shouting his greetings to Connor and waving him inside all at the same time.

No Edwardian lace for Jordan today, Connor noticed. And no jacket and tie, either. The boy was wearing a sweater and jeans, and clearly enjoying it.

Maggie heard the doorbell from the kitchen. Nervously she untied her apron, and then changed her mind and did it back up again. In spite of what Connor's mere presence did to her, she was determined to be as natural as she would be with any other friend who'd been invited for a meal.

The problem was, none of her other friends happened to have the kind of good looks that made a woman's heart turn over, and none of them had ever looked at her with the kind of gaze that she met when she went into the foyer to greet Connor. The gray tweed jacket he was wearing accentuated his broad shoulders, and something about the understated red of his tie reminded her of all the passions smoldering just below the surface of her mystery man—passions she was all too willing to answer.

She wanted to cross the tile floor to him and give him a hello kiss, if only to have the excuse to touch him. But with Jordan in attendance, showing affection for Connor took on a different meaning. And just as well, she reminded herself. She was far from comfortable with Connor's secretive streak. Inviting him to dinner was one thing, but giving any of her emotions into the charge of a man who wouldn't even tell her his last name was something quite different.

"You look wonderful," he was saying, and Maggie was glad she'd put on another of her comfortable "old favorites"—a loose-fitting cotton-jersey dress that had once been much brighter, but which had faded over the years to a warm, goldenrod yellow. She'd gathered the dress at her waist with a casual woven-fiber belt and ornamented the simple round neckline with a strand of wooden beads she'd had for years.

It was funny, she thought. She'd seldom worn these things during her marriage. As Grant's wife, she'd felt she should dress as the other people in his immediate circle did, and she'd bought fancy dresses and conservative suits accordingly. Connor seemed to remind her of things she'd thought were long forgotten.

"You look pretty dashing yourself," she told him, thinking he was the last person she'd ever expected to see in a suit.

"You didn't have to wear a tie, though," Jordan chimed in, and Maggie was grateful her son had said it for her. "We only have to dress up when we go to Grandma's. Mom didn't even make me brush my hair before I answered the door, like she usually does."

"I usually do that because otherwise you'd never brush your hair at all," Maggie told him. A glance at Connor's neatly combed hair made her think of their embrace on the windy seashore, and the way his tousled locks afterward had seemed to sum up their tangled feelings.

"Anyway, you don't have to keep your tie on," Jordan was continuing irrepressibly. "Mom won't mind."

Connor was grinning down at the boy. "That's good to know," he said, amusement creasing the small laugh lines at the corners of his eyes. "But I might as well stay dressed up for a while, since I've made the effort."

He transferred his smile to Maggie, and she felt her knees weaken. The man had no right to be so attractive, or to fit so handily into her home like this. The careful distance she'd been hoping to keep was shattered by their first shared smile.

"Why don't you come and keep me company in the kitchen?" she suggested. "I just have to fry the tortillas, and then we can set the table."

"The living-room table, right, Mom?" Jordan asked anxiously.

"Sure, honey."

"The dining-room table's only for fancy guests," Jordan explained to Connor. From the look on Connor's face, Maggie thought, he didn't mind being included in the category of nonfancy company.

"Tortillas for Sunday dinner?" he said, leaning his hips against her kitchen counter as though he'd done it a thousand times. "And here I was expecting a standing rib roast."

"I should have warned you we were being a little informal," she said, smiling. "I hope you don't have your mouth all set for meat and potatoes."

"My mouth is set for whatever you've got cooking right now," he said gallantly. "What's in that pot?"

Maggie hadn't forgotten his prowess as a chef, and she'd hauled out her favorite recipe to do him justice. "It's a special secret tomato sauce," she said. "I learned it from the Mexican cook at the house where my mother used to be the maid. And the other pot has spiced ground meat in it. We're having a do-it-yourself sort of meal," she added, turning on the heat under her fryer, "and I hope you like things hot and spicy."

"Of course," he said smoothly, and she was saved from wondering if he intended a double meaning by the ringing of the telephone on the kitchen wall. She reached for it, still watching Connor's handsome face.

"Hello?" she said. "Oh, Mrs. Blake. Hello. How nice to hear from you."

She was aware of the change in her own voice as she spoke. The informal Maggie of a moment ago was replaced immediately by the well-heeled young woman she'd become under Mrs. Corviser's expert tutelage.

She was aware of something else. Connor's face had frozen, and his smile was gone. *What on earth?* she thought as she listened to old Mrs. Blake's question. How could a simple change in Maggie's tone of voice turn Connor off so completely?

"I'm sorry," she said into the receiver. "She's gone to New Haven for the weekend, and I don't expect her back until tomorrow morning. If he's that insistent about it, maybe I should give you the number of the friend she's staying with."

Connor's face was like a granite mask, and even Jordan seemed puzzled by it. "Hey, Connor," he was saying uncertainly. "Want to come and see my dinosaurs?"

Connor held out a hand. The gesture was so brusque that Jordan subsided into silence, and they both listened to Maggie finish her conversation.

"I'm so sorry. What does the doctor say? Yes, I suppose even someone as stubborn as Mr. Blake is going to have to acknowledge that sooner or later. But it must be very hard for you. Are you sure you don't want me to let Caroline know? Well, I'll be happy to do it if you change your mind. Take care, now, Mrs. Blake. Goodbye."

She'd barely hung up the phone before Connor pushed himself away from the counter with one motion of his strong thigh muscles. "Come on, Jordan," he said curtly. "Let's go look at your dinosaurs."

Maggie was left gaping at his sudden disappearance. She started to go after them into the living room, but something told her Connor wouldn't welcome her company. She shut her mouth with a click and went back to the stack of corn tortillas on the counter. Cooking was at least predictable, she thought, although climbing Mount McKinley in snowy weather was probably predictable compared to figuring out Connor.

She could hear his deep voice talking to Jordan, so at least he hadn't withdrawn completely. She finished cooking and started carrying bowls and platters into the living room, and by the time she'd arrayed the wide coffee table with an appetizing buffet of sauces and condiments, Connor seemed to have become almost civil again.

Almost. She could still feel the tension radiating from him, although he was clearly making an effort to disguise it. At least his appetite wasn't impaired, she thought, watching him heap meat, sauce, lettuce, sour cream and cheese on his first stack of tortillas. Her own stomach felt tightly knotted, constricted by the idea that she could be so powerfully attracted to a man who was proving to be more of a mystery every time she saw him.

"This is wonderful," he said, around bites of his dinner. "Best Sunday dinner I've had in years."

"What do you usually do for Sunday dinner?" she asked, impelled by curiosity. "Do you have family in the area?"

"None to speak of. I usually spend Sundays in my shop, tinkering with new ideas."

"What kind of ideas?" Jordan wanted to know.

"Well, kiddo, I take it as kind of a personal challenge that there are thieves out there who know how to get past every kind of lock there is. So I've spent a lot of time over the years trying to come up with things they *can't* get past."

"For cars, you mean?" Maggie asked.

"Mostly for homes," he replied. "I've come up with some pretty tricky little devices, if I do say so myself."

Maggie was thinking of the security system he'd had thoughts of marketing someday, and the big Marblehead estate where they'd been last week. Several times in the past few days she'd had thoughts of jumping in her car and driving back to Marblehead Neck to look at the name on the gate, but every time she'd restrained her own curiosity. It seemed more important to hear the whole story from Connor himself. She was sure he cared for her, but did he care enough to be completely honest with her?

"It's funny," she mused. "Here you are, as footloose and fancy free as anyone I've ever met. Even your kitchen has four wheels, for heaven's sake. And yet you spend your spare time making people's nice, secure houses even more secure."

"It is funny, when you put it like that," he said slowly. And then, as though the question followed logically from what she'd said, he asked, "What was the crisis on the telephone a little while ago?"

Maggie sighed as she thought about it. "Just one in a series of ongoing crises, I'm afraid," she said. "I'm sure you'd find it very mundane."

"Maybe not." He sounded casual, but as though he was working hard to be that way. "You looked pretty worried about it. I was just wondering what happened."

"It's a long story," she hedged, and then Jordan took over, clearly impatient with his mother's roundabout way of getting to the point.

"It's Uncle Blake," he said. "I call him Uncle Blake, even though he isn't related to us. He and my grandfather started a company together, about a hundred years ago."

"Almost," Maggie corrected, smiling. "The firm just had its forty-fifth anniversary. It's the company I was telling you about last week, Connor. We call it Triple I, in the family."

"The firm your husband worked for." His voice was oddly flat.

"Yes. Working for Triple I is sort of a tradition for both the Lewises and the Blakes. At least, it has been up till now. The firm is going through a tough time at the moment."

"First of all my father died," Jordan said, matter-of-factly. "And last year my grandfather died. And now Uncle Blake is sick."

"He has a very bad heart," Maggie explained. "And he's, well, he's a very stubborn, old man. He sees that the old ways are changing, but he can't come to terms with it, I'm afraid."

"What do you mean?"

There was no mistaking the genuine interest in Connor's tone, although Maggie couldn't imagine why their family business should be so riveting for him. "Mr. Blake feels that nobody but a Blake or a Lewis should be running Triple I. The problem is, his only son isn't interested in the company, and there's no one else left to do it."

"He doesn't have any other kids?"

"A daughter, but she's not interested in investments. She works for the company, in the personnel department, but she doesn't want to take over the whole show."

"I can't say I blame her. It sounds pretty dull," Connor muttered, almost to himself.

"My dad didn't think it was dull," Jordan said, reproachfully.

"I guess it's one of those things that either grabs you or it doesn't," Maggie went on. "Apparently the Blakes' son went to work for Triple I when he got out of college, but it didn't grab him enough. He left when he was in his early twenties."

"There was a big fight," Jordan added.

"Really?"

Connor seemed barely interested by now, Maggie thought. He was paying awfully close attention to his dinner.

"Uncle Blake said if his son wouldn't work for Triple I, then he couldn't be his son any more," Jordan said.

Maggie smiled at her son's evident enthusiasm for the story. "It's become sort of a family legend, I gather," she said. "It gets told and retold at all the family gatherings, which is the only way Jordan knows of it. Or me, for that matter."

"So you never met the renegade Blake."

"No. I haven't even seen a picture of him. His father literally struck him from the family records, photographic records included."

"Seems pretty harsh."

"Well, Mr. Blake is a stubborn, old man."

"And now he's . . . unwell?"

There was something in the question that made Maggie raise her head, but Connor was still looking down at his plate. "His doctors say his heart can't last much longer," she said. "It's hard for him, seeing the company he's run for so long being turned over to people who aren't family."

"Most businessmen aren't so sentimental," Connor observed.

"Most businesses aren't like Triple I," Maggie countered. "It's still very much a family-run affair."

"I remember you said you were a board member."

"She doesn't like it," Jordan said, looking from Connor to his mother.

"Don't you?"

Now they were both looking at her. "Not really," she admitted. "I'm one of those people who definitely isn't grabbed by the investment business." She smiled, trying to turn it into a joke, but Connor wouldn't let it end there.

"Then why do it?" he demanded.

"It's . . . part of the deal," she said. "Something I married into." Her words sounded lame, she thought, and wondered how her bowing to tradition must strike a rebel like Connor.

"Like Sunday dinners at the Lewises," he was saying. "And The Stearns School."

"Yes," she said, feeling defensive now. "And what's wrong with that?"

He didn't seem to want to answer the question. "What about you, Jordan?" Connor transferred his glare to the boy, who was building a second stack of tortillas and sauce. "Are you going to work for Triple I when you get older, just like your father?"

Jordan shrugged. "I might," he said. "Or I might be a magician. I haven't decided yet."

There was no hint of a smile on Connor's face. "Well, I have no doubt you'll be a major shareholder, either way," he said. "Your husband must have had considerable stock in the company, Mrs. Lewis."

Why on earth was he so angry and formal, all of a sudden? He'd reverted to being the aggressive intruder of his first visit here.

"He did," she admitted, "and most of it is in Jordan's name. I'm keeping it in trust for him, along with the rest of his inheritance."

"All for Jordan?" he queried. "None for you?"

She looked down at her plate, wishing he'd stop questioning her. "You may already have gathered that I'm not completely comfortable with wealth, Mr.…Connor. I prefer to earn my own keep, which is one of the main reasons for my day-care center. Everything else will go to Jordan some day. My job is just to manage it until then."

They both looked at her son, whose rumpled brown head was bent over his meal with total absorption. At least Jordan would grow up used to the idea of having money, Maggie thought, and with any luck she could raise him to use it responsibly.

"It's a lot to ask of a kid, isn't it?" Connor asked unexpectedly.

She met his eyes. "Yes," she said, "but no harder than asking a child to be poor."

That seemed to set him back. "I suppose," he said. "What I meant was, it's unfair to ask a child to fit into someone else's plans. You might as well be manufacturing a series of robots, if all you want of your children is a younger version of yourself."

She couldn't miss the bitterness in his face. It was clear that they weren't talking in abstracts here. "I can't imagine anyone trying to shape you that way," she ventured.

His bark of laughter wasn't even slightly amused. "Oh, I can imagine them trying it," he told her. "Fortunately, I can't imagine them succeeding." He looked abruptly at his empty plate, and then around the table. "I've managed to clean you out of sour cream," he said, "and I think I've still got room for one more tortilla. Let me refill the bowl."

"I can do that," Maggie protested, as he got to his feet.

"No," he said forcefully. "Just tell me where it is."

Once he'd escaped to the kitchen, it was a few minutes before he even looked in the refrigerator. He was annoyed to find himself shaking inside, with the age-old rage and frustration that the thought of his father always caused. He'd had no business to let himself get this involved with Grant's widow. And yet to walk away from Maggie and her son now would be a gigantic wrench. He thought of the taste of Maggie's lips with the salt spray on them, and the restless dreams that had kept him company for the past week.

Being a loner had been all right up till now. But now it wasn't good enough any more. He wanted to be with Maggie, to share her life, to know the secrets those dancing golden eyes could teach him. If it meant facing his father again, he'd just have to do it. Connor squared his shoulders and headed back into the living room, remembering at the last moment the sour cream that had been his excuse to grab a moment by himself.

Around the table, he found a serious conference going on. "We've decided," Maggie informed him, "that you'd be much more comfortable without your jacket and tie. We voted unanimously that you can take them off if you like."

Connor had to smile at that, although he wondered if he'd been such a surly beggar that they thought they'd better placate him. Gratefully he loosened his tie, and miraculously, his mood did seem to improve. The end of the meal was relaxed and even boisterous, as Jordan attempted to display his racing cars amongst the empty plates and bowls on the table.

When things threatened to get out of hand—with Connor making a ramp out of the leather cushions from the sofa, and small cars hurling themselves through the atmosphere—Maggie suggested a walk. "The flowers are just blooming," she said, "and the Arnold Arboretum is always a good place for a walk."

"Oh boy!" Jordan said. "Dog shopping!" He raced off to get his coat.

"Dog shopping?" Connor raised a thick brow at Maggie as he helped her clear the plates and bowls from the table.

"Half of Boston seems to bring their dogs to the Arboretum for a walk on Sunday afternoon," she explained, smiling. "And Jordan's been pestering me to get a dog for a couple of years. I haven't given in yet, but he likes to think that whenever we go to the Arboretum for a walk, we're really shopping to find the kind of dog we want."

"Why don't you get him his own dog?"

"Because I know perfectly well who'd end up taking care of it. Jordan's at school all day, and there's always something extracurricular going on there in the evenings. Having a dog and going to a place like The Stearns School just aren't compatible, I'm afraid."

"Why don't you send him to a regular public school?" His tone was belligerent.

Maggie made herself stay calm. She was beginning to resent Connor's insistent prying into her private affairs. "Because he's getting an excellent education where he is," she replied.

"And because it's traditional, right?" He was putting things into the dishwasher now and seeming to take out his unexplained anger on her china.

"Partly, yes. What's wrong with that?"

"It just bugs me to see a kid forced to grow up according to someone else's pattern, that's all." Connor knew he was sounding unreasonable, but he couldn't banish the memory of the small rebellious boy he'd once been, and how the life Jordan was leading now had grated on him.

"You may not have been one of them from the beginning," he went on, not looking up, "but you've really bought the program now, haven't you, Maggie?"

"One of 'them'?" she demanded. "Who's 'them'?"

"You know." Connor waved a hand, oblivious to the china bowl he was grasping. "The Lewises. The Blakes. Those families you married into. You may have started out as the maid's daughter, but you're pure old money now, aren't you?" He used the bowl to sketch a motion of disgust.

Maggie refused to let him see how his words hurt. "If I am, that's my choice, and none of your business. And be careful with that bowl. It's part of the old china my mother-in-law gave us for a wedding present."

He gave a mirthless chuckle. "See?" he said. "I knew there was a traditional Sunday dinner lurking just under the surface. It may have been Mexican food, Maggie, but it was still served in the ancestral china, wasn't it?"

Maggie stared at the top of his jet black head, completely mystified by him again. She knew his words were way off the mark, but she sensed that somehow they weren't really directed at her, but at some hurt in his own life.

"Look at me," she commanded, her voice low. After a moment's hesitation, he did, and she could see the turmoil in his eyes without having the slightest idea what had caused it. It made part of her want to smooth away the trouble on his face. The other part of her wanted to boot him on his admittedly attractive posterior until he started making sense.

She didn't do either of those things. Instead, she almost whispered, "Who are you, Connor? Why won't you tell me?"

The anger in his eyes melted in an instant, and he looked almost weary. "I'll tell you soon, I promise," he told her.

"Why not now?"

He sighed, and straightened from his position in front of the dishwasher. "Because it's a nice spring day," he hedged, "and we're going for a walk, and Jordan is all excited. I don't want to ruin that."

"Is your secret that bad?" she couldn't help asking. "This can't go on, Connor. I keep imagining all sorts of terrible things, like you're a hunted criminal or a—"

"Don't." He stepped toward her and closed the distance between them in a split second. Before she could go on, he covered her lips with his hand, gently, almost sensually.

Almost nothing. His movement grew into a caress as soon as his flesh met hers, and Maggie responded to it. Connor's arm encircled her waist, and she felt his warmth through her yellow dress. His other hand moved from her lips to trace the contours of her face as though he was memorizing her. Then he ran his fingers through the soft curls framing her face.

"Don't push me yet," he muttered, with his lips against her hair. The words were an entreaty, not a demand. For the first time Maggie could sense a vulnerable inner core to her handsome, freedom-loving vagabond. Irrationally, it made her trust him a little more.

She could feel the warmth of his breath now; he was devastatingly close. Both of them were trembling, shaken by a desire that Maggie found almost shocking. Nothing in her wild teenage years or her brief marriage to Grant had prepared her for this instinctive passion, this glad abandoning of herself into a realm where rules and reasons didn't matter.

Connor's lips were grazing hers, and she barely heard him say, "Don't imagine too many terrible things about me, Maggie. Try imagining what you and I would feel like together instead."

His kiss was a mere shadow, and she tilted her face up-ward to follow its path. His voice was rough with yearning, and smooth with certainty. "I've been imagining it ever since I met you. Have you?"

"Yes." It was impossible to hide the truth, especially when he claimed her so possessively and so fully. Their embrace joined the lengths of their bodies with an intimacy that made Maggie forget who or where she was, and she answered the pleasing thrusts of his tongue with demands of her own, demands that Connor fill all her senses and make them overflow...

"Aren't you guys ready yet?"

The sound of small feet clattering down the staircase jolted her back into reality. Connor released his grip, and Maggie stepped back from him, stunned as much by the sudden end of the whirlwind as by the fact that she'd allowed herself to be swept up in it.

"We'll be there in a minute, honey," she called out, wishing she sounded steadier. "Why don't you wait in the car?"

"Looks like we've got ourselves a chaperon," Connor commented. She could see his broad chest rising and falling as he struggled to get his breathing under control. He was rolling down the sleeves of his white shirt, trying to seem at ease.

"Maybe that's a good thing," she replied.

He looked up, a hint of a grin in his eyes. "Are you saying you don't feel quite safe with me, Mrs. Lewis?"

She rolled her eyes, exasperated with the man. "What's not to feel safe about?" she asked, leading the way to the front hall. "Just because I've known you for two weeks and you still haven't told me your last name?"

"Picky, picky," he teased, and ran a hand appreciatively over the curve of her hip before she put on her conservative tan trench coat. "You keep concentrating on the inessentials."

It was clear what he considered to be essential, and the annoying thing was, Maggie thought, that half the time she was inclined to agree with him. The taste of his mouth, the heat of the passion that always ignited between them— maybe those things were more important than a mere formal introduction, after all.

"Just remember, you promised to tell me your secret eventually," she reminded him, clinging to sanity in the face of overriding desire.

"I remember," he said gravely. "But not today."

"Not today," she echoed.

Connor shrugged into his gray tweed jacket and stuffed his Sunday tie into a pocket. "Come on, then," he said, putting an arm around her. "Let's go dog shopping."

Five

They had a tough time deciding on a dog. Connor favored big, burly types that reminded Maggie of the hound of the Baskervilles. She inclined more toward small ones with intelligent faces. Jordan was as fickle as always, favoring any and every dog that licked his face or let him pat its head.

"Maybe we could get *two* dogs," he said, as they retraced their steps toward the quiet side gate where Maggie had parked the car. "A small one for you, Mom, and one of those hairy ones for me."

"Good try, Jordan." She mussed his hair affectionately. "You're going to have to get pretty proficient with the vacuum cleaner before you can talk me into getting an Old English sheepdog."

"Oh, well." Jordan sounded philosophical, and Maggie wondered if the enlisting of Connor as an ally in the dog campaign was going to bolster her son's efforts to talk her into a pet.

"What about a nice cat?" she suggested.

Jordan made a face. "Cats don't fetch," he said succinctly, and then ran ahead of them to greet a wolfhound fully two inches taller than himself.

Maggie and Connor sauntered behind him, hand in hand as they'd been for most of their hour-long walk. Even this casual contact kept reminding Maggie of the tug of their mutual attraction, and she'd been glad of the distractions that Jordan and his incessant dog-hunting had provided.

"You don't work on Sunday nights, right?" she asked him, wondering if it would be wise to prolong his visit over supper.

"Right. A guy's got to have some kind of weekend."

She smiled at the thought. "'Some kind' is one way to put it," she said. "Considering you got home at seven this morning—"

"And went straight to bed, like a good boy." Connor grinned at her. "So I got a good five hours' sleep before I came over for dinner."

"Or breakfast."

"Or whatever."

They were laughing by now, even though Maggie was still wondering how such a crazy schedule could ever mesh with the routine life she led herself. "Don't you ever wish you kept the same schedule as the rest of the world?" she asked.

"Hell, no. I've always been fond of turning things upside down."

That was exactly what he did to her, and he knew it. She could see it in his eyes, and the curve of his lips only confirmed it.

"Well," she said, and was about to take the plunge and invite him to stay to supper. But before she could go on, he stopped suddenly, like a hunting dog listening to a rifle shot in the distance.

"Did you hear that?" he demanded.

"I didn't hear anything. What was it?"

"Listen."

His voice was as tense as the rest of him. Maggie stood still next to him, listening hard, and thought she heard a faint sound like someone dropping a glass on a tile floor.

She hadn't had time to make sense of the noise before Connor took off, sprinting like an Olympic athlete as he called over his shoulder, "Come on!" Easy for him to say, Maggie thought. His powerful muscles had carried him out of her reach by the time his words came back to her. She scooped up Jordan and jogged quickly to where her car was parked.

When she reached the cul-de-sac, it was only too clear what Connor's sharper ears had heard. Three vehicles lined the road—her own, another car and a pickup truck whose door was swinging open, obviously the victim of vandalism.

And not the only one. Maggie saw with a gasp that broken glass lined the street in front of the two cars, and realized that someone had smashed the headlights. She sighed angrily, maddened by the senseless destruction.

Sharp, staccato footsteps caught her attention, and she looked up to see Connor walking back toward them. His own anger was evident in his stride. "I saw them," he said, breathing hard. "But I couldn't catch them. Three little hellions with a hammer, which they probably stole from that pickup."

A glance inside the burgled truck revealed a toolbox with its lid open, and Maggie sighed again. First her stolen purse, and now this. The time it took to deal with the police and the insurance company was almost worse than the vandalism itself.

"There's a pay phone back inside the gate," she said wearily. "Do you want to call, or shall I?"

In the end, all three of them ended up walking back to the pay phone and then waiting by the car for the police to arrive. By the time the patrol car pulled up in the cul-de-sac, the owners of the other vehicles had arrived as well. That translated into more standing and waiting while the police took down everyone's information and tried to figure out exactly what was missing and damaged. Maggie could see Connor's growing impatience as the policeman asked him for the third time to give a description of the vandals he'd barely seen.

"I don't like to complain," Jordan said, as the sun started to sink behind the trees, "but I'm getting kind of hungry."

Maggie rubbed her son's head affectionately, grateful for his ever-calm manner. "I know, honey," she said. "I hope we'll be done soon."

It was almost dark, though, by the time they got back to Wellesley. While they were climbing out of the car, Maggie was struck by a thought.

"I won't be able to drive at night, will I?" she said. "Not without headlights."

"It won't take long to fix," Connor said. "Just stay at home for an evening or two."

"I can't." Maggie turned to him, wondering if their relationship had reached the stage yet where she could ask him a favor. "My sister-in-law is coming back from London tonight, and I'd promised I'd pick her up."

"Let her take a cab."

The gruffness in his voice made her hesitate. "I'd suggest it, if I had any way of reaching her. But she'll be expecting a ride, and I hate to make her wait."

She left the favor unasked, hoping he might offer a ride of his own accord. If he didn't, she'd just have to improvise.

"I guess there's no way you can get away with driving the car this way," he said slowly, looking at the smashed headlights.

"Maybe a daredevil like you would try it, but I'm not about to," she said firmly. "I just paid the ticket I got the last time I went to the airport; I don't think I'll start collecting any more."

He was silent for so long that she was sure he was searching for a polite way to beg off. "It's all right," she said hastily. "I'll think of some way to get there."

"How?"

"I don't know yet. Take a cab myself, I guess."

His grin seemed forced. "I thought you rich folks hated wasting money on cabs," he said.

Her frustration with him spilled over then, and she felt her temper starting to fire up again. "If I hear one more crack about rich folks from you," she said evenly, "I'm going to suggest that you put one of your own locks on your mouth and throw away the key."

He looked startled. "No need to be mad," he said, although he'd egged her on to it himself.

"No," she agreed coolly. "You're right. There is, however, a need to get some food into Jordan and start getting ready to get to the airport somehow, because I don't have a whole lot of time to get this done."

Feel free to take your leave, her manner said clearly, but for some reason he wasn't taking the hint. "Relax," he said, following her to the front door. "I'll take you to the airport."

"There's no need—"

His hand on her shoulder was suddenly aggressive, and the look on his face wasn't one she wanted to argue with. "I said, I'll take you to the airport," he repeated, with a squeeze of her shoulder for emphasis. And then, as though she wasn't mystified enough already, he muttered half to himself, "It would have happened sooner or later anyway." With that cryptic remark, he ushered her in the door.

Maggie kept a tight grip on her purse from the moment she entered the international terminal, and an even tighter grip on Jordan's hand. It didn't leave her a whole lot of gripping power left for her temper, and she was feeling angrier than ever with Connor, even though he'd obligingly ferried them directly to the door.

"Why was Connor so quiet all the way here, Mom?"
Jordan wanted to know.

She didn't have an answer for him. She couldn't begin to
explain Connor's moodiness to herself. "I think he must
have had something on his mind, honey," was the best she
could do.

"It was funny," Jordan said seriously. "He says he's
going to drive us home to Wellesley again, but he doesn't
seem to want to."

"Sometimes you're pretty smart for a kid, you know
that?" And far too observant, she wanted to add. "Maybe
Connor's just tired. He works such crazy hours."

Fortunately, her explanations seemed to satisfy Jordan,
if not herself. And fortunately Bobbie's flight was on time,
and before long Maggie could concentrate on watching the
passengers coming through the sliding doors, instead of
tormenting herself with questions about Connor.

Bobbie's red hair was easy to spot. Grant's hair had been
a gentle auburn, but his more flamboyant sister had always
enhanced the family coloring to a coppery red that made her
stand out in a crowd. Ironically, next to her sister-in-law,
Maggie felt like the pampered daughter of old money that
Connor had accused her of being just this afternoon. Bobbie, on the other hand, would never have been taken for a
member of the wealthy, conservative Lewis clan.

"Maggie! I'm so glad you're here. I've got tons of luggage, you won't believe it." Maggie was momentarily swal-
lowed up in a hug. "I missed you, sweetie. And you, too,
little pal." She transferred the hug to Jordan.

"I hope you don't mean literally tons," Maggie said, and
explained about her car. "A friend gave us a lift, but I'm not
sure how many clothes he can fit in the back of his van."

"Not to worry. I'll perch on top of them if I have to.
Maggie, the clothes in London are sensational. Wait till you
see the fall display I'm going to put together."

Like Maggie, Bobbie had elected to earn her own keep
rather than live on the Lewis family money. Chez Bobbie,

her shop in Quincy Market, was a thriving concern, so much so that Bobbie had treated herself to a first-ever buying trip to London this spring.

"Even you are going to love these dresses," she was going on, as they waited for her baggage at the carousel. "We've got to jazz up your wardrobe, sweetie."

Maggie eyed her sister-in-law's tight black pants and short lime-green bolero jacket doubtfully. Her jersey dress appeared outdated by comparison, but then Connor hadn't seemed to mind when he'd run his hands along her waist and hips in the kitchen this afternoon.

What was Connor doing now? He'd seemed in such a black mood when they'd left him at the curb. Maggie almost hesitated to face him again, and yet she had the feeling that some sort of crisis was approaching. Whatever was on his mind, she'd rather know about it than feel all at sea every time she encountered him.

The solution to the mystery was almost absurdly simple. Once they'd collected Bobbie's bags and trunks and loaded them into a towering pile on a luggage cart, it didn't take long to trundle everything outside to the curb. The navy van was there, with "K.C's All-Night Locksmith" emblazoned on its side, and Bobbie's eyes widened at the sight of it.

"Aren't you the sly one?" she asked Maggie, not taking in her sister-in-law's confusion. "I thought that man was never going to set foot inside the family circle again."

And before Maggie could demand to know what she meant, Bobbie had caught sight of Connor lounging in the driver's seat and crossed to meet him. "K.C. Blake!" she said, greeting him with a warmth that he made no attempt to return. "Probably the last person I expected to see."

"It's a bit of a surprise for me, too, Bobbie," he said tightly. Maggie could tell he was avoiding her eyes.

"Well, I'm much obliged for the ride," Bobbie was continuing. "I'm about beat. I take it you remember the way to the old homestead, K.C.?"

"How could I forget?" His answer came from between clenched teeth. He slid down from the van and moved to the luggage cart as though he wanted to get this over with but couldn't quite bring himself to participate in the reunion.

Maggie stayed on the curb while the others stowed Bobbie's luggage in the back of the van. So Connor was one of the Blakes, the renegade son who'd caused all the upheaval in the clan! It explained so many things—his personal interest in her affairs and his strong feelings about the Blake family fortunes. No wonder he hadn't wanted to go into this with her. Having the secret finally out in the open didn't help to clear up the future, at all.

"I'll sit in the back," she volunteered, as she saw Connor starting to close the van's back doors.

"No need, sweetie." Bobbie was already clambering over the mountain of luggage. "Since I dumped all this stuff on you, the least I can do is sit in the back with it and catch it if it topples over. Want to help me, Jordan?"

And so Maggie found herself climbing reluctantly back into the front seat beside Connor. He was silent, his handsome face glowering at the dashboard. Maggie tried to meet his eyes, but after one brief glance he looked steadily forward, not at her.

Bobbie continued to fill the silence with chatter as they left the parking lot and headed for the expressway. "I'd appreciate some warning if we're going around any sudden corners, K.C.," she said wrapping an arm around her pile of suitcases. "This stuff's sort of heavy. And boy, do I ever remember your driving!" She turned to her sister-in-law. "Has K.C. told you about the night he drove Grant and me down to the Cape, and we nearly went over a cliff?"

"Actually, he's been very modest about his past," Maggie said pointedly.

Connor finally faced her, and he looked trapped and angry. "I don't go by K.C. any more, Bobbie," was all he said. "My name's Connor now."

"Fine by me," Bobbie replied. Either jet lag or Bobbie's effervescent character must be blinding her to the tension in the van, Maggie thought. "Although it's a bit confusing when people you grew up with start using different names, all of a sudden."

Connor seemed to be in no mood for effervescence. "I've been using it for fifteen years," he said bluntly.

"Has it been that long since you...left? I suppose it has. Makes me feel old."

Maggie was afraid there would be nothing left of Connor's teeth if he clenched them any harder. To give him a break from Bobbie's innocent but barbed questions, she said hastily, "Tell us about your trip, Bobbie. How did you like London?"

"London was fantastic, really a lot of fun. And you'll never guess who I saw there, K.C.—I mean Connor. Do you remember Elliot Masters, who used to go out with Jacquie?"

"Vaguely."

"He and his wife were there, sightseeing. I ran into them in Trafalgar Square, of all places. I gather he's been doing some business with Triple I. He was asking me how your father was doing."

Connor's silence was so pronounced that even Bobbie couldn't miss it. "How *is* he doing?" she asked, less confidently.

"The last time I saw him he was spitting nails and trying his damnedest to work himself into another heart attack," Connor said grimly. "And I suppose there are people who would tell me it was my fault."

"Oh." With that uncharacteristic monosyllable, Bobbie gave up on the conversation, and chatted quietly with Jordan for the rest of the trip.

Maggie was grateful for the respite, although she knew the storm was far from over. Once they'd dropped Bobbie at her coach-house apartment behind the big Lewis home, and put a sleepy Jordan to bed upstairs at Maggie's house, there were still a hundred things to be sorted out between her and Connor. And she was dreading it, as she closed her son's door and walked softly back downstairs to the living room.

He was standing in front of the fireplace when she entered, one arm stretched on the mantel and his head down so that she couldn't see his face. It was like confronting a stranger, as though the appealing bohemian she'd been so bowled over by had vanished. She didn't know what to say to this silent, embittered man.

Then he tilted his face toward her, and her heart beat faster when she saw the familiar rakish grin on his lips. "Still talking to me?" he asked, almost casually.

"Still listening to you, is more like it," she told him. "You've got a lot of talking to do, Connor."

"I did promise you I'd get to it sooner or later, didn't I?"

How could that grin be so seductive? Maggie found herself drawn toward him, nestling herself into his open arms before she'd thought about what she was doing.

"Things would have been simpler if you'd just told me the truth at the beginning," she murmured, letting herself be pulled against his white shirt front. Through the thin cloth she could feel his heart beating in an escalating rhythm that matched her own.

"Do you really think so?" He kissed her hair, and then her earlobe, as though he was bent on arousing her in spite of anything she might say. "I would have said nothing could be simpler than this, than what we feel for each other."

As if to prove it, he kissed her gently, not probing or demanding, but touching her lips so invitingly that Maggie couldn't help but respond. Connor's caresses never failed to light an inner fire in her that she seemed powerless to resist.

At first she simply revelled in his touch, knowing that this could only complicate the problems they had to resolve. But the gentle pressure of his mouth was too enticing, and she found it harder to remember her reasons for staying aloof. She parted her lips and felt his kiss grow in intensity, meet-

ing her own desire halfway and making the blaze inside her
burn a little more fiercely.

His tongue explored the warm cavern of her mouth with
a gentle thoroughness that made her head spin. Somehow,
she knew for a certainty that his lovemaking would be just
this thorough, this slow and maddening. His hands slid
from her shoulders down to the curves of her back and
thighs, and back up again over her flat stomach and the
roundness of her breasts. Briefly he paused to circle their
taut centers, and then moved on, leaving her gasping for
more.

See? his slow caresses seemed to be telling her. *See what I
can do to you?* And the hell of it was, she thought, that she
did know. And she wanted all of it.

"Connor, this isn't fair," she breathed, when he finally
lifted his head. His eyes were utterly black, as fathomless as
the sea, and she had never seen that look of passionate need
on a man's face before. The hardness of him, as he pulled
her against his body, made her certain that his need was as
real and insistent as her own.

"Who said anything about fair?" he demanded. His voice
was rough, but somewhere deep inside it that seductive grin
still lurked. "I want you, Maggie. And unless I'm very
wrong, you want me too."

Again he brushed his palms over her breasts, looking
satisfied and stirred at the same time when he called up a cry
of delight from her throat. "I want to know all of you," he
murmured, kissing the base of her neck where the turmoil
in her blood betrayed itself by its throbbing. "Every inch of
your skin, every part of you that needs to be satisfied. I
dream about you every night, Maggie. I dream of doing just
this."

In one smooth motion he had lifted her from her feet, and
carried her to the broad leather sofa where they'd sat to eat
their Sunday dinner a few hours before. It had been arousing enough to sit next to him then; it was nearly unbearable

now, when his strong upper body pushed her down among the cushions and her mind swam with images of the two of them making love.

The images became real, as Connor ran a knowing hand along the inner length of her thigh. She was aching for him, arching to meet his touch, and when he skimmed his fingers over the scanty lace panties she wore, the hunger inside her became even more immediate and fierce.

"I knew your skin would be this soft," he said. There was pleasure in his voice and in his touch as he explored the curves of her stomach and hips. "Just like satin that's been worn next to a woman's skin a thousand times."

His words stirred her imagination, and she opened her eyes slowly. There was an open adoration on his face that shook her, and went far beyond her experience of how a man could love a woman. His eyelids were lowered, as he seemed to drink in the sight and feel of her. His hands gave her pleasure everywhere they touched.

Desire made her bold, and she raised her own hands to caress his face, the lips that could switch so disarmingly into his rogue's grin, the heavy, dark lashes that hid his eyes. She let her hands follow the strong lines of his neck and shoulders, and heard him give a groan as she drew her fingers over the sprinkling of black hair at the vee of his open shirt collar.

"Oh, God, Maggie," she heard him say. Something in his tone awoke the part of her that was half in love with the sense of freedom he gave her, with the way he seemed to reach out to the woman she'd been long before she'd learned to fit into the lives of the wealthy.

That thought brought her upright with a jolt. Connor moved with her, still pinning her in his arms. "Maggie, what is it? What's wrong?"

She had to stop while she was still in control, before the blaze inside her burned her common sense into a charred nothingness. "Damn you, Connor Blake, *this* is wrong, and you know it," she said shakily.

"How can it be?" He was running his fingers through her hair, returning to his earlier gentleness. "How can anything that feels this good be wrong?"

She escaped from the embrace that was stirring her so devastatingly, and stood up. Her legs were as shaky as her voice, but she knew she was doing the right thing. She refused to let any man, even one as attractive as Connor Blake, throw her entire life into chaos just for one evening of passion.

"You do have a way of distracting attention from the real problem," she told him, thinking of how he'd always been able to make her forget herself with his kisses.

"And what's the real problem?" He was sitting up straighter now, still fighting to get his breathing under control. Some of this evening's wariness was creeping back into his eyes.

"In the first place, I wouldn't feel right making love down here on the sofa like two teenagers while my son sleeps upstairs. It's just—"

"Respectable, young widows don't do things like that, right?" His grin was mocking her, but she welcomed the anger it sparked.

"*I* don't do things like that, and if that makes me a respectable widow, so be it." She crossed to the fireplace, turning her back to the solid red bricks as though they could give her support. Inside she was still churning with uneasy desire. "And in the second place, there are things we have to work out, Connor, before we—"

"Hop into bed," he finished bluntly.

"If you want to put it that way, yes. I'm not interested in a quick fling, Connor."

"Neither am I." His teeth were clenched again, she noticed.

"Well, that means you would have to fit into my life somehow, doesn't it? Sunday dinners, school committees, going to Triple I board meetings—that's the world I'm part of, like it or not."

"I can't do that," he said. "I've cut myself off from all of that."

"You could come back," she said softly. "At least part way."

"No." The word startled her with its ferocity. "Don't even ask that, Maggie. And why should I be the one to do the fitting in? Why don't you consider fitting into my life, instead?"

Maggie had to laugh, without much amusement. "That seems pretty likely, doesn't it?" she asked him. "With a seven-year-old in school, and a day-care center to run. How on earth could I fit into your schedule, when you get home from work about the time I'm getting out of bed?"

"Well, I guess you're right, then. We do have problems." He put his locked hands behind his head, glaring at her. "If you're not willing to part with any of these nice things." He nodded his head at the oak paneling and leather furniture.

"Stop it!" Maggie said, suddenly angrier with him. "I wish you'd stop trying to make me out to be some little gold digger who married into the Lewises to get at the family fortune. It wasn't like that."

There was a long silence as they assessed each other. Finally Connor said more gently, "What was it like, then?"

Maggie sank into the upholstered chair next to the unused fireplace, wondering if she could possibly make him understand. They'd come from such different backgrounds, and had both run full tilt away from their roots. How could they have any common ground, now?

"My father left us when I was five," she said simply, starting at the beginning. "He'd always fancied himself as a minor entrepreneur, and he kept investing his money—*our* money—in things that always went belly up. When he'd pretty much cleaned out what resources we had, he disappeared. My mother and I were pretty hard up, and since the only skills she had were cooking and cleaning, that was what she did to support us.''

"Being a maid," he supplied.

"Yes." She felt a spurt of the old resentment. "I'm sure you know about those, Connor. You must have grown up with a couple around the house." She made herself stay calm, and went on. "I told you we lived in Newark, in a tough neighborhood. I was in a bad school, with a bad group of kids, and getting wilder by the minute, as far as my mother was concerned.

"When I was twelve, she decided I needed a better place to grow up. She took a live-in job for a rich lady, Mrs. Corviser, in Westchester County. It didn't have much effect on me, at first. I still managed to find the roughest kids to hang out with, and by the time I was fourteen I was every mother's worst case scenario.''

"Up to and including lifting Mrs. Corviser's jewelry," Connor supplied, when she paused.

"Yes. I thought she was going to turn me in, but she must have seen something in me that she liked, because instead she ended up taking me under her wing. She was almost eighty then, and had no kids of her own. Maybe that was why she did it, I don't know. Anyway, she decided I was going to be a lady, and that was it.''

"She did a good job," Connor commented.

"She was a very determined woman. And a very smart one. She taught me about clothes and manners and which fork to use for my salad. And I turned out to be a very good student. I figured out pretty fast that this was my ticket out of the kind of life my mother was leading—washing pots and pans in other people's kitchens.''

"Where is your mother now?"

"She died ten years ago, of cancer. She never seemed to mind waiting on rich people, the way I did.''

"Is that why you decided to become one of them?"

"I didn't decide it, Connor. I fell in love with Grant, and we got married. It was that simple. Since then I've met a lot of rich people that I didn't like, but I've also met some that I liked very much, including the Lewises and the Blakes. I realized how stupid it was to classify people according to how much money they had. And since I had the tools to fit into this kind of world, it wasn't hard to do.''

"I congratulate you. Your disguise is nearly perfect."

"Nearly?" She spoke sharply.

"Yes. You forget that I've had lots of opportunity to study the genuine article. I grew up surrounded by women who had the kind of background and manners that you've learned to imitate. And you do it very well. But there's still something about you that's, well, different."

That was just what Maggie herself had always felt. No matter how hard she tried, she was never completely at home in the world of wealth. "No one's ever complained about it before," she said lightly.

"Oh, I'm not complaining. It's one of the things I find so damned attractive about you."

He sounded as though he wished he *didn't* find her so attractive. "Thank you," she said, a trifle coolly. "You have a delicate touch with a compliment. Well, that's my life story, Connor. Don't you think it's time you told me yours?"

He exhaled slowly and let his arms down from behind his head. She could see him fighting against her suggestion, and finally bowing to the inevitable. Abruptly, he stood up, and walked to look out the window at the dark night. His back was toward her, and all she could see of his face was the shadowy reflection in the small panes of glass.

"I was supposed to be what Grant was," he said bluntly. "Presentable and well-behaved and dedicated to International Investments, Incorporated." He shoved his hands deep into his black trousers. "Needless to say, I wasn't. I wanted to travel, to have adventures, to be my own person. That never went down well with my father, and the older I got, the more rigid he got. A childhood phase was bad

Yes, become a Silhouette subscriber and the celebration goes on forever.

To begin with we'll send you:

4 new Silhouette Desire® novels — FREE

a lovely 20k gold electroplated chain—FREE

an exciting mystery bonus—FREE

And that's not all! Special extras— Three more reasons to celebrate.

4. FREE Home Delivery! That's right! We'll send you 4 FREE books, and you'll be under no obligation to purchase any in the future. You may keep the books and return the accompanying statement marked cancel.

If we don't hear from you, about a month later we'll send you six additional novels to read and enjoy. If you decide to keep them, you'll pay the low members only discount price of just $2.24* each — that's 26 cents less than the cover price — AND there's no extra charge for delivery! There are no hidden extras! You may cancel at any time! But as long as you wish to continue, every month we'll send you six more books, which you can purchase or return at our cost, cancelling your subscription.

5. Free Monthly Newsletter! It's the indispensable insiders' look at our most popular writers and their upcoming novels. Now you can have a behind-the-scenes look at the fascinating world of Silhouette! It's an added bonus you'll look forward to every month!

6. More Surprise Gifts! Because our home subscribers are our most valued readers, we'll be sending you additional free gifts from time to time — as a token of our appreciation.

FREE! 20k GOLD ELECTROPLATED CHAIN!

You'll love this 20k gold electroplated chain! The necklace is finely crafted with 160 double-soldered links, and is electroplate finished in genuine 20k gold. It's nearly 1/8" wide, fully 20" long — and has the look and feel of the real thing. "Glamorous" is the perfect word for it, and it can be yours FREE in this amazing Silhouette celebration!

SILHOUETTE DESIRE®

FREE OFFER CARD

4 FREE BOOKS

20k GOLD ELECTROPLATED CHAIN—FREE

FREE MYSTERY BONUS

PLACE YOUR BALLOON STICKER HERE!

FREE HOME DELIVERY

FREE FACT-FILLED NEWSLETTER

MORE SURPRISE GIFTS THROUGHOUT THE YEAR—FREE

YES! Please send me my four Silhouette Desire® novels FREE, along with my 20k Electroplated Gold Chain and my free mystery gift, as explained on the opposite page. I understand that accepting these books and gifts places me under no obligation ever to buy any books. I may cancel at any time for any reason, and the free books and gifts will be mine to keep!   225 CIS JAY9 (U-S-D-02/90)

NAME
_____
(PLEASE PRINT)

ADDRESS _____ **APT** _____

CITY _____ **STATE** _____

ZIP _____

Offer limited to one per household and not valid to current Silhouette Desire subscribers. Terms and prices subject to change without notice. All orders subject to approval.

© 1989 HARLEQUIN ENTERPRISES LTD.

SILHOUETTE "NO RISK GUARANTEE"
• There's no obligation to buy — the free books and gifts remain yours to keep.
• You receive books before they're available in stores.
• You may end your subscription anytime — just by letting us know.

PRINTED IN U.S.A

Postage will be paid by addressee

BUSINESS REPLY CARD
FIRST CLASS   PERMIT NO. 717   BUFFALO, N.Y.

SILHOUETTE BOOKS®

901 Fuhrmann Blvd.,
P.O. Box 1867
Buffalo, N.Y. 14240-9952

FILL OUT THIS POSTPAID CARD AND MAIL TODAY!

NO POSTAGE
NECESSARY
IF MAILED
IN THE
UNITED STATES

enough, but he refused to have a son who wasn't interested in the family business. Refused."

The word had hurt as well as anger in it, and Maggie could sense how much Connor must have wanted to have his father accept him for himself.

"I did all the right things. I went to The Stearns School. I got my bachelor's degree at a fancy college. I went to work at Triple I, just like Grant had done. And then when I was twenty-two, something snapped. I couldn't do it any more. I couldn't be the way they wanted me to be."

"And so you left." Maggie had heard the story many times, from Connor's family and from Grant, who'd always been a little hurt and puzzled that his boyhood friend had left so suddenly.

"I ran away to sea." She could hear the faint amusement in his lowered voice. "Sounds romantic, doesn't it? But I did it—and every other crazy romantic thing that came into my head. I drifted all over the place till I was nearly thirty, and then I drifted into a job in New York City, as an all-night locksmith. It was the perfect job for someone as rootless as I wanted to be. Lots of challenge, and a fair bit of danger, too."

"From more than just bounced checks, I take it."

"From things you probably already know about, if you grew up on the tough side of Newark. There's lots of punks out there who think anybody with a van and a wallet is worth rolling. I thought I was pretty tough from working cattle ranches in Wyoming, but let me tell you, New York at three a.m. was a lot tougher, yet."

"What made you come back to Boston?" she asked softly.

He shrugged, and turned to face her. "Damned if I know," he said. "First Grant died. That shook me up. He was only two years older than I, and we'd always been as close as two such different people could be. For him to die so suddenly, and so young..." He turned his palms up, and

Maggie nodded. She knew only too well the disbelieving sense of loss he was talking about.

"And then old Mr. Lewis died, and things started to look bad for Triple I's future. With Grant dead and Bobbie not interested and my sister Jacquie not wanting to take over, my father decided I was the only hope for the firm." Maggie shared his ironic smile as she imagined what that confrontation must have been like. "He didn't try to break it to me gently—just called one day and informed me I'd been indulging myself long enough, and it was time to come home and take over the reins."

"That must have gone over well," she said.

"Right. Like the proverbial lead balloon. I dug in my heels and determined to stay with my job in New York for the rest of my life. And I might have done it, too, if Dad's heart hadn't gotten so bad."

Maggie remembered all too clearly the panic of four years ago, when Kincaid Blake's first massive heart attack had happened. "He was pretty scared," Connor said, and Maggie could see in his face the same strong lines as his father's—the face of a man who hated to admit he might be beaten. "He asked me to come home. Asked, not demanded, and I did it. I moved my business here, and decided I could compromise, for the sake of keeping the family together at a time when we all needed each other."

"I remember your mother was so sure you were going to come back and work for Triple I, when you moved back to the area," Maggie said.

"Well, she was wrong." Connor's eyes were hard. "I've done what I said I would do. I'm here now, the way my family wanted. But I'm not giving up my freedom for that damned business, no matter who asks me to do it."

With a sudden chill, Maggie realized that his words were aimed directly at her. She was so closely involved in his family's affairs; did he see his involvement with her as a threat to his independence? Maybe it was, she thought glumly.

"What did Grant tell you about me?" His question came out of the blue, and she realized he must have been wanting to ask it for a long time.

"That you were as loyal as they came," she said, recalling Grant's exact words. "That you and he had grown up like brothers. And that he was sure you'd come around some day, and turn out the way your father wanted. Grant was very...traditional," she added, feeling she should soften her last statement.

Connor's eyes were full of conflicting feelings, and she could hardly bear to look into them. "There's not much you could tell me about Grant, Maggie," he said. "Well, that's my life story, as requested. Where do we go from here?"

"We can't go back," she said, wishing she could comfort away the strain on his face. But she had tension of her own to deal with. "We can't pretend any more that I don't know who you are."

"No. And I can't rejoin the happy family circle, either. My father foams at the mouth at the sight of me these days."

Maggie knew it was a fairly accurate description. "Then what?" she asked, throwing the ball back in Connor's court.

"We could carry on in secret." He seemed to be testing her.

"No. Any 'carrying on' I do has to include Jordan."

"Fair enough. We could wait for my father to die, I suppose."

"You don't mean that."

"Don't I?" The exaggerated hardness of his voice told her he was forcing himself to seem callous, hiding what he was feeling inside. "Well, anyway, my father's such a stubborn old man, he'll probably last for years in spite of everything the doctors tell him. Seems to me we're out of options, Maggie."

His eyes were pleading with her, asking her to find some middle ground. The trouble was, she couldn't see any. She was committed to her life and the responsibilities that came with it. And Connor was just as committed to avoiding it.

"We could call it quits, I suppose," she said, her eyes swimming with sudden tears.

"When we're so right together?" he demanded.

The memory of lying beneath him on her sofa, with her body and soul alive to the touch of his fingertips, made her tremble. But she held firm to her resolve. "In some ways we aren't right together, at all," she told him. "I'm sorry, Connor. Maybe there's just no way to work this out." The words turned the trembling inside her into an ache that was almost pain.

"You know what you sound like right now?" he was demanding, grabbing his jacket from the back of the sofa. "You sound just like my mother telling one of the servants they're fired. Very polite and so sorry, but underneath it all it doesn't mean a thing to her. It's just a matter of business. Is that how you feel about me, Maggie?"

"Do you think it is?" Maggie was stung by his words.

"I wouldn't put it past you. You learned your lessons well, didn't you? Mrs. Grant A. Lewis, Jr. regrets that the pleasure of Mr. Blake's company will no longer be required. Thank you so much."

There was such venom in his "Thank you so much" that Maggie didn't even try to contradict him, and by the time she'd thought of a reply, he had slammed out of the living room and through the front door. She waited, keeping the traditionally stiff upper lip until she'd heard his van's engine receding into the distance, and only then did she allow herself to cry.

Six

_____

"Would you like more coffee, Mrs. Lewis?"

"No, thank you, Cindy."

Maggie smiled at the Blakes' maid. She'd never gotten comfortable with having people serve her food, the way the Lewises and Blakes clearly were.

She looked around the table, surveying the other guests at Mr. and Mrs. Blake's wedding anniversary dinner. No one else was noticing Cindy at all, let alone smiling at her. It was ironic, Maggie thought, that in standing firmly against Connor's attractions and electing to stay a part of this close-knit family group, she'd actually made herself feel more of an outsider than ever.

At the head of the table, old Kincaid Blake was holding forth on his favorite subject: the future of International Investments, Incorporated. "Anyone who can't see that the Japanese market is the next place to move has their head in the sand," he was saying. "I've been saying that for years."

"We believe you, Dad," his daughter Jacquie replied. She was a slender woman a couple of years older than Maggie, whose shoulder-length black hair framed an almost always serious face. Her husband, Richard Westborough, sat beside her, and together they looked like the perfect portrait of a young professional couple.

Across the table, Bobbie's flamboyant, short yellow dress was just the right yin to their yang, Maggie thought. Jordan sat next to his mother, in his Sunday jacket and tie. The two older women, Mrs. Lewis and Mrs. Blake, rounded out the dinner party, looking elegantly calm as they almost always managed to do.

Only one family member was missing, although he was never far from Maggie's thoughts these days. And before long, he'd made his presence felt in the conversation, as well.

"There's no point to making big plans for expanding," Kincaid Blake was grumbling, "thanks to that brother of yours."

Jacquie sighed. "Let's not talk about it now, all right, Dad?"

"Why not?" the old man demanded. "I'm sure you all talk about me when I'm not around. Why shouldn't I do the same for that boy?"

"'That boy' is thirty-seven years old, dear," Mrs. Blake reminded him. "I really think you should get used to the idea that he knows what he's doing with his life."

"Knows what he's doing?" Connor's father snorted. "I've seen that tin can he drives around in. That's no vehicle for a Blake to be driving, not if he knows what he's doing."

Maggie met her sister-in-law's eyes across the table, and Bobbie seemed to understand the silent plea to change the subject. "It may be a bit banged up," Bobbie said, "but it carried five trunks of clothes home from the airport the other night, so I can't complain about it. And speaking of clothes—"

She launched into a description of the fashion previews she'd attended in London. Kincaid Blake was still frowning from the head of the table, like the fierce old patriarch he was, but at least the awkward subject had been dropped for the moment.

Maggie and her mother-in-law sat on the same side of the big table, with Jordan between them. As the others chatted of London and fashions, Caroline Lewis leaned over Jordan's shiny head and said, "Maggie, you're looking awfully tired. Are you working too hard these days?"

Maggie managed a smile. "I don't seem to be sleeping very well," she admitted. "It must be the spring air or something." *Or Connor Blake*, she added mentally, thinking of all the hours she'd spent this past week lying awake and thinking of him, first with longing and then with anger, and then with longing again.

"Well, whatever it is, you're looking very pale. I worry about you and that day-care center. Looking after six children every day can't be an easy thing."

Maggie was about to frame the polite reassurance she'd given Caroline so many times before, when the Blakes' maid stepped into the dining room and provided a welcome interruption.

It was only welcome until she spoke. Looking at Mrs. Blake, Cindy announced, "Mr. Connor, ma'am."

"Thanks, Cindy." Maggie could hear his deep voice before she could see him. "You're one of the few people around here I've convinced to use my real name instead of my initials."

Then he was in the room, and Maggie felt her breath catch in her throat. He was wearing a brown turtleneck, black trousers, and a dark brown corduroy jacket that looked brand new, and he was immediately the most vital person in this well-bred gathering. He stepped forward to kiss his mother.

"Happy anniversary, Mom," he said warmly.

"Thank you, dear." She stood to greet him. "I'm glad you came."

"How the devil did you know we were having dinner?" Kincaid Blake demanded. Maggie winced at the harshness of his tone.

Connor seemed remarkably calm. Maybe he'd known what to expect. "Mom called and invited me," he said evenly. "Said she was sure you'd be pleased if I came."

"Hmph." Maggie had never heard anyone who could pack more contempt into a wordless snort. "I thought I made it clear, the last time you chose to show yourself here, that the only way I'd be pleased to see you was if you changed your mind about coming back to the firm."

"Please, dear—"

Mrs. Blake's words overlapped with Connor's reply. "It's a bit soon to start fighting, isn't it?" he asked equably. "Let's finish celebrating your anniversary first." He strode to the head of the table and held out a hand. "Congratulations on forty-five years."

Maggie could see Connor's hand shaking slightly, despite his calm words. Confronting his father must be a gut-wrenching task. Then why had he come?

It took a long time for Kincaid Blake to offer his hand in return. "Thanks," he said gruffly. "Couldn't be bothered wearing a shirt and tie, I see."

Connor's jaw tightened. "Well," he said, with an obvious attempt to keep cool, "I figured if I did, you'd probably complain that it wasn't a tux. So I decided to wear what I'm comfortable in."

"Story of your life," the old man muttered. "Always out to please yourself."

He seemed determined to pick a fight, and Richard interrupted to prevent it. "It occurs to me that introductions may be in order," he said hastily. "Maggie, I don't think you've ever encountered Jacquie's brother, have you?"

For the first time since he'd entered the room, Connor turned to look at Maggie. And instantly she was lost in the depths of those impossibly dark eyes, just as she had been from the beginning. She could feel the warmth of him from across the room.

"As a matter of fact, we *have* met," Connor was saying gravely. "Hello, Maggie. Hi, Jordan."

"Hi, Connor. You know what? We went to the park last night and I saw the most awesome kind of dog."

"Is that right?" Connor pulled up a chair and set it between Maggie and her son. "What kind was it?"

With a united sigh of relief, the guests around the big table followed Jordan's lead and went back to chatting of small things. The maid brought the silver coffee pot around again, and the sunlit, glassed-in dining room seemed a little brighter.

The weather was hinting at summer, and before long the Blakes' guests started getting up from the table and drifting out to the lawn, where there were already daffodils nodding in the gardens and hints of leaves on the trees.

Connor made no move to get up, and Maggie stayed seated beside him, hoping that they might have a chance to talk in private. That seemed to be on his mind, too, because when they were finally alone at the long table he turned to her with an unmistakable hunger in his eyes.

"I thought we were going to have to wait all afternoon for them to leave," he said.

"Your mother fed us too well, as usual," she said, smiling. "We were all too full to move."

"I'd forgotten about my mother's meals." He grinned at her. "I haven't been home for many lately, as you may have gathered."

As always, that grin disarmed her and made it impossible to think about anything but touching him. Hesitantly, she reached up and pushed a lock of his thick, black hair back from his forehead. His sudden intake of breath told her the simple gesture affected him as much as it did her.

"It must be very difficult," she said softly. "Having your father be the way he is, I mean."

"It is difficult." His grin twisted into something bitter, and then faded altogether. "But it's a picnic compared with what I've gone through this past week, Maggie."

"What—what do you mean?"

"I mean being without you, wondering if you'd ever want to see me again."

He leaned forward in his chair, running his strong fingers through the hair at her neck and massaging the skin beneath. "You left so suddenly," she said, wondering if he knew what his touch was doing to her. "I wasn't sure what to think."

"I've always bolted from things that made me mad," he confessed.

"Like you did when you were twenty-two?" She thought of the life story he'd told her last Sunday night.

His face hardened as she reminded him of it, and he stopped massaging her neck. "Yes, like that," he said. "And now you've seen for yourself what I was running from."

"I already believed you, Connor," she said. "Is that why you showed up here today? Just to prove a point?"

In fact, Connor had shown up because he didn't think he could survive one more day without a glimpse of Maggie. But they didn't seem to be at a point yet where he could admit that to her. "Maybe," he hedged.

"That doesn't solve anything, does it?" she persisted.

He stood up restlessly. He'd grappled with this problem all week, and he knew she was right. "I guess not," he said, shoving his hands into his pockets and staring moodily out onto the lawn where an impromptu game of croquet was being set up.

Maggie stood too, wishing she could physically sweep aside the obstacles that seemed to divide them. "Things were so straightforward before, when I thought you were just an all-night locksmith without a last name," she mused.

He turned, almost angrily. "They were straightforward because of one thing," he told her. "I wanted you, and you wanted me. Has that changed, Maggie?"

His dark eyes seemed to drag the truth from her. "No," she admitted softly, and was about to take three steps closer to him and prove it when the outside door to the dining room opened and Connor's father entered.

"Your mother seems to think you should be out enjoying the sunshine," he said.

The old man's timing never *was* very good, Connor reflected. "I hate croquet," he said bluntly.

"So do I. Pointless game." Kincaid Blake seated himself again at the head of the table. There was no doubt where Connor had gotten those glaring, dark eyes, not to mention his strength of character, Maggie thought. "And speaking of pointless games—"

Connor knew what was coming next. "Do we have to go over this again?"

"We'll keep going over it until you give in," his father replied. Maggie could almost see the sparks flying between them.

"Well, I hope you're not holding your breath. Triple I is going to have to look to someone besides me for its new president."

"Damn it, boy, there isn't anywhere else to look!" Kincaid's anger was tinged with desperation, and both Maggie and Connor heard it. "Do you want to see Triple I run by strangers?"

Maggie could see Connor trying to conquer his anger, and she admired him for it. She sensed him trying to be reasonable about this whole emotional issue, perhaps for the first time. Maybe, between that and Kincaid's obvious feeling of urgency, they might actually be open to a compromise. She stayed silent, watching them.

"They wouldn't all be strangers," Connor was saying. "The people who run it now are people who've worked for you for years. They're good, trusted executives."

Kincaid gave his snort again. "Of course they are," he admitted grudgingly. "But that doesn't mean they have the same feeling for the firm that a family member would have."

"Why can't you just accept the fact that I *don't* have that kind of feeling for Triple I?"

"Because I know you, boy." Kincaid leveled his most penetrating stare at his son, and Maggie was glad she was out of its range. "You make a big deal about being independent, but deep down you're as much a Blake as any of us. Don't try to deny it."

To Maggie's infinite surprise, Connor *didn't* try to deny it. Then she remembered what he'd said about coming home when Kincaid had had his first heart attack four years ago—that being together with his family meant a lot to him. Maybe the future of Triple I mattered, after all. Maybe it was just the terms of Kincaid's demands that were keeping him so aloof.

"I'm just not cut out for that kind of life," Connor was saying. "And don't tell me I haven't tried it. I gave it a two-year trial, and that was plenty long enough to know that putting on a suit every morning and going into the office wasn't for me."

"Two years!" The old man was clearly contemptuous now, and Maggie had a feeling that a major fight was brewing. "Two years, when you were barely out of school. Hardly what I'd call a fair trial."

"At least I didn't just write it off, like you've done with the career I've made for myself," Connor shot back.

"Career! More like a hobby, if you ask me."

There was too much hurt and anger on both sides for anything good to come from this, Maggie knew. Quickly she stepped between the two tall men, and held up a placating hand.

"Please," she said. "Yelling about it isn't going to help."

They both turned those belligerent stares on her, and it was like stepping under a hundred heat lamps. But she went on calmly, "Isn't there some sort of middle ground, Mr. Blake? Something else that Connor could do at Triple I, without committing his whole life to the company?"

"You make it sound like such a duty, girl. Hell, I committed *my* whole life to the company, and—"

"But Connor doesn't want to," she pointed out. Kincaid looked surprised that she'd interrupted him, and she was a little surprised herself. She always been a bit intimidated by Connor's father before this. "Maybe if you just accepted that fact, you two could work something out."

The glance they exchanged was far from comfortable, but at least it was better than yelling. "What are you proposing?" Kincaid asked gruffly.

Maggie hadn't gotten that far yet, and she scrambled to come up with a peace accord they might both go for. "Well, what about some sort of position on the board of directors, where Connor could have a say in company policy without having to be in the office all the time the way you've been?"

"Hmm." The senior Blake was actually looking thoughtful. "I'd have to think about that."

"And that way it wouldn't take all of your time," she said, turning to Connor and hoping he might see some glimmer of hope in her scheme.

"Great idea, Maggie." The sarcasm in Connor's voice caught her off guard. "How much of my life are you planning to sign away for me? You want to take over my business for me while I'm busy at Triple I board meetings?"

"Of course not. It's just the first compromise that came into my head, that's all. And if there's one, there could be others. If you're really interested in coming to terms—"

Connor didn't let her finish. "I'm interested in living my own life on my own terms," he informed her. "And I might have known all your high-minded talk about staying loyal to the family was just a cover for trying to rope me into this."

"What are you talking about?" Kincaid was frowning again, at both of them.

"Maggie and I were trying to come to some terms of our own," Connor said, "but it seems I've wandered back into the same, old argument without realizing it."

Maggie clenched her fists at her sides. "That's unreasonable, and you know it," she shot back at him. "I'm not trying to rope you into anything. All I want is what's best for the whole family—"

"And Triple I," he interjected.

"Yes, because that's part of the family. And so are you, no matter how hard you try to avoid it. Your father's right about that, at least."

There was a long pause, and Maggie held her breath while praying that Kincaid wouldn't say something belligerent to break Connor's silence. Miraculously, he didn't.

When Connor finally spoke, all the anger had gone out of his voice. "Of course I'd feel happier if we could come to some agreement," he said. "I just think we need to do some hard thinking about it, that's all."

"You're right there, boy." Kincaid rapped the dining-room table with his knuckles, the way he always did at Triple I board meetings when things needed calling to order. "And thank God, thinking is one of the few things I'm still perfectly capable of doing. Why don't we go into the study, where they won't be pestering us to play croquet, and maybe we can come to terms."

Once again Maggie hardly dared to breath for fear of breaking the mood. Connor's eyes met hers, briefly, and she saw in his face how much the possibility of being reconciled with his father meant to him.

"I'll go make excuses for you at the croquet game," she said lightly. "See you later, Connor."

But by the time the game was over and the warm day was growing chilly again, the two men still hadn't emerged from Kincaid's study on the second floor. And Maggie, for all she wanted to see Connor again, wouldn't have disturbed them for the world. She heard Mrs. Blake giving Cindy instructions to set Connor's place at the table for supper, and smiled as she took her leave with Jordan and her mother-in-law. She still had no clear idea of what the future might hold for her and Connor, but at least she was certain that it wouldn't be dull.

"And to think I once wanted to have six kids of my own!" Maggie muttered, hastily swallowing two aspirins. "They should issue industrial-strength earplugs to anyone who's crazy enough to start a day-care center."

Chaos reigned in the playroom at the back of her home. It was a gloomy, wet April day, and either the low atmospheric pressure or the fact that the kids hadn't been able to play outside had turned them into small tornadoes. Maggie had tried all her usual rainy-day diversions, but nothing had worked. She had six bored children on her hands, and it was about to drive her nuts.

"Why *can't* we go outside?" one of them asked, for what seemed like the hundredth time.

"Because it's raining too hard," Maggie explained, less patiently than she had the previous ninety-nine times.

"My mom lets us play outside when it's raining," said the child.

"Your mom only has to clean up after one of you," Maggie said. "By the time you all got your raincoats on, it would be time to go home, anyway."

And it would, thank heavens, she thought, looking at her watch. Both her reliable teenage baby-sitters were away on a school trip this week, and Maggie was having to cope on her own instead of having help after three o'clock. It was nearly five now, and before long the parents would be coming to pick up their kids. *And good luck to them*, Maggie thought fervently.

She knew her state of mind had more to do with Connor Blake than anything the six children had been up to. She had been thinking about him constantly since yesterday, wondering what had gone on between him and his father and when she was going to hear from him again. She'd lain awake for much of last night, listening to the pelting rain and imagining vividly enticing things about Connor.

There was a pounding at the door of the playroom, and Maggie jumped. "Coming!" she called, wondering which parent was so annoyed by the weather that he or she was knocking so loudly.

It wasn't a parent. Connor stood on the doorstep, dripping wet and huddled into his old, brown leather bomber jacket. His eyes, looking at her from beneath those heavy black brows, were as riveting as ever.

"I tried the front door," he explained, "but no one answered. This is quite a party you've got going here, Maggie."

"It's cabin fever," she said, above the noise. "Usually I take them outside and run them around a bit. It tuckers them out. But today I couldn't do that. Give me your coat," she added, stepping around the six whirling dervishes in the room. "The parents should be here any minute. We can talk once the kids are gone."

He shrugged out of his jacket, and she carried it to the front hall. Normally she would have draped it over the chair in her office, but today she was seizing any opportunity for a quick break from the pandemonium in the playroom. Connor had cost her a nearly sleepless night, she thought tiredly. Let him work that off by giving her a minute's peace today.

She couldn't help lingering a moment as she hung up his old jacket in the hall cupboard. It smelled so much like him. It even *looked* like him—rugged and well-traveled and showing the scars of long experience.

Somehow, miraculously, that experience must have included some time spent with kids, because when she got back to the playroom she found Connor had organized an impromptu game of pick-up sticks. The noise level had dropped several decibels, and she could hear herself think for the first time all day.

"I tried pick-up sticks about two hours ago," she said reproachfully, "but they weren't interested."

"You didn't make it worth their while," Connor said, deftly maneuvering one stick under another. "We're playing for pennies, aren't we, kids?"

Maggie looked at the pile of pennies on the floor next to Connor's knee. "Uh, Connor," she said, "I don't usually include gambling in the day's activities."

"Come on, Maggie." He flashed her that devil-may-care grin. "It's only pennies."

On the one hand, Maggie hoped the children didn't go home with tales of winning money playing pick-up sticks at day-care. On the other hand, the room was blessedly quiet now, with all six youngsters concentrating their hardest on the wooden sticks. Maggie sighed and decided to turn a blind eye.

Most of the parents arrived at five-twenty, exclaiming about the weather, and Maggie was kept busy hustling children into raincoats and boots and hats. By the time five of the children had gone, it was quarter to six, and the pick-up sticks game was officially over.

Connor and the last remaining child seemed to have disappeared, she noticed. Well, they couldn't have gone far. She went into her office, thinking that she really did need to make a rule about parents who were late picking up their kids. As she entered the small room, she felt a suspicious draft at her ankles.

"Connor?" she called, stepping back into the playroom. "Is the front door open?"

There was no answer, and she went into the front foyer to investigate. Sure enough, her front door was standing wide open, and crouched down in front of it were Connor and the three-year-old boy whose parents hadn't shown up yet.

"What are you doing?" she asked, frowning at the two of them.

"Nicky wanted to know how to pick a lock," Connor said.

Several questions came to Maggie's mind. "Why do you want to know how to pick a lock, Nicky?" she asked helplessly.

"My big sister locks her room when she goes out," the boy said, with a grin all too reminiscent of Connor's. "She won't let me see what she's got in there."

"Maybe she hasn't got anything in there," Maggie suggested, gently but firmly pushing the front door shut. "Maybe she just wants her privacy. Did you think of that?"

"It's all right, Maggie," Connor interposed. "I already pointed that out to him. I was just showing him that locks aren't that easy to pick anyway, so he shouldn't waste his time trying."

Maggie had to smile. "There's the back door. That'll be your mom, Nicky. Let's get your coat on." She turned to face Connor who was looking far too amused by something. "I'll be back in a minute," she said.

By the time Nicky had gone, Jordan was home and announcing in the same breath that he was starving and that he had to be back at the school at seven-thirty for a debating contest.

"Oh, Lord," Maggie said, following her son into the kitchen. "Sometimes I think our car could probably find its way to The Stearns School without me driving it, Jordan. It seems to go there at least three nights a week."

Connor had seated himself at the kitchen table and was looking very much at home. At the sight of the big man, Jordan's face lit up. "Hi, Connor!" he said. "Mom didn't tell me you were coming."

"Mom didn't know," Maggie said. "Are you staying for dinner, Connor?"

"Sure," he said. "I have to go to work early tonight, so I'll have to leave about seven-thirty myself."

"Hey, that's right. This is first thing in the morning for you, isn't it, Connor?" The fascination of Connor's all-night job caught Jordan's imagination all over again.

"You bet. Actually, I wasn't angling for a dinner invitation. What I really came for was a few words alone with your mother."

Jordan, sensitive beyond his seven years, immediately took the hint. "I was going upstairs to practice my speech," he said, on his way out of the kitchen. "Call me when dinner's ready, okay?"

"Okay," Maggie promised, adding, "once I figure out what dinner's going to be, that is. These evening events at school really throw my schedule off."

She put a big pot of water on the stove to boil, and opened the refrigerator, hunting for possible leftovers that could be converted to a topping for pasta. To her surprise, Connor stood up, turned the burner off, pushed the refrigerator door closed and reached for the telephone on the wall.

"What are you doing?" she demanded.

"I said I came for a few words with you," he said, "and I don't intend to share your attention. Where do you usually call out for pizza?"

With his free arm he encircled her shoulders, and Maggie let herself be pulled against his broad chest with a startled laugh. "Don't tell my mother-in-law that we ever do any such thing," she said, "but it's Domenic's Pizza Parlor." She gave him the number.

While Connor ordered a large pizza with the works, to be delivered, Maggie gave herself up to the pleasure of being this close to him again. He was wearing his usual working clothes—blue jeans and a heavy, navy blue sweater—and when she put an arm around his waist, the flesh beneath her fingers felt springy and responsive. She closed her eyes, caught up in imagining how that strong body would feel against hers. When Connor was in a good mood, as he was now, it was so tempting to give in to her fantasies about the man.

But there were still problems to resolve, and she suspected that was what he'd come to talk to her about. It made her wary of getting carried away by her feelings for him, and she tried to keep her voice calm when he'd hung up the phone.

"I was wondering why you were here," she said. "I thought maybe you just stopped by to corrupt a few nice, respectable Wellesley children."

"That wasn't the reason, but I have to admit I had fun doing it," he admitted with a grin. "Did you really think I was going to teach Nicky to pick a lock?"

"Well..."

"Admit it, Maggie. The look on your face when you came into the foyer gave you away. You thought I was starting that kid on a life of crime."

"Or at least getting him into serious trouble with his big sister."

"I wouldn't have done it, you know."

"I know. And anyway, you may have saved my sanity by showing up when you did."

"Always glad to oblige." The smile on his face faded a little, and he pulled her against him with a sudden hunger. "Always glad to see you, too. I'm sorry my meeting with my father went into overtime yesterday. I was hoping to get a chance to talk to you before you left."

"I didn't want to interrupt you," she said. Connor's nearness made her short of breath in an entirely pleasant way, and her whole body seemed to spring into quivering life in his arms. She reached for him, twining her arms eagerly around his broad shoulders. A tremor ran through his frame as she fit herself more closely into his embrace.

Then his mouth captured hers, and the familiar wave of longing swept her away from everyday life. His lips probed and caressed, awakening feelings she hadn't known existed before he had brought them to light. The longing for him was nearly unbearable, and when his searching hands cradled her breasts it was all she could do to repress a gasp of delight.

"Connor," she managed, breathlessly, "this is crazy."

"I agree."

She could feel him shudder again as he shifted his grip and pulled her so tightly against him that she knew unmistakably how much he wanted her. He was covering her face with kisses now, leaving her aroused and alive wherever his lips touched her skin. He pushed aside the oversized collar of her shirt, and slowly, sensuously nuzzled the line of her collarbone. It was like hooking up a direct current to her pulsating inner core, and Maggie's sudden intake of breath proved it.

"We have to stop meeting like this," he said raggedly, lifting his head and burying his fingers in her thick, tawny hair. "Why is it there's always somebody around when we're together?"

It certainly seemed to be true, Maggie thought. Every time the passion between them flared, there was a handy chaperon somewhere nearby. She was peripherally aware of Jordan, studying upstairs in his room, and she knew it was the wrong time to be getting carried away by Connor's caresses. Still, when she felt his warm breath so close to her ear...

"And if there's nobody around, then we seem to be fighting about something," she added, hoping that uncomfortable subject might calm things down a bit.

It didn't. Connor only flashed a smile at her, and that unnervingly attractive grin got to her, as it always did. This time it was Maggie who initiated the kiss, tangling her fingers in his jet black hair and lifting her lips to his as though she'd been thirsty all her life and had just discovered a wellspring in Connor Blake.

Her passion added fuel to his, and reality threatened to fade away again for Maggie, until she vaguely heard her small son's voice floating down the stairs.

"Mom? What time's dinner?"

She forced in a deep breath and Connor loosened his grip slightly. "As soon as the pizza deliveryman gets here, honey," she called back.

"We're having pizza? Oh, boy!"

She took advantage of the interruption to move to a safer spot, one where Connor's touch wouldn't threaten to overturn the entire order of the world as she knew it.

Connor reseated himself at the kitchen table, arms across his chest, and Maggie thought he, too, looked as though he was trying to calm down the desire that had boiled up inside. "Good timing, huh?" he said, with a faint echo of that rebel's grin.

"Wonderful," she replied. "I know what you mean about us never having any uninterrupted time together."

"All that was missing was for the pizza to arrive."

He glanced at her kitchen clock, and seemed to decide it was time to get down to business. "Maggie, this really is crazy. I barely sleep any more, thinking of you, wanting you."

His words had almost the same effect as his touch. Her heart was still pounding as she listened to him.

"Can't we arrange to spend some time together—alone? I mean, I'm as much of a family man as anyone, but..."

He let his words trail off, his meaning only too clear. He ran a hand through his hair, pushing it back from his forehead, and Maggie followed the gesture with her eyes. She could almost feel her fingertips in his thick, black hair, and it made her realize just how hungry she was for everything Connor's lovemaking could give her.

Were they ready to take that step? She needed to know, first, what had gone on in Kincaid's study yesterday afternoon.

"Are you really that much of a family man, Connor?" she wondered out loud.

"Sure I am. Jordan and I get along just fine. I've always liked being around kids."

That was clear enough. He'd been having a ball this afternoon, down on his knees in her playroom with the pickup sticks. "That wasn't what I meant," she said. "I was thinking about your family. What happened yesterday, after I left?"

"Something about as momentous as the laws of gravity being repealed, as far as the Blakes are concerned," he said, smiling. "My father and I actually agreed on something."

Maggie knew just how momentous that really was. "Come on, Connor, you're keeping me in suspense," she said. "What did he say?"

"Well, he thought your idea had some merit in it. About me taking over the chairmanship of the board, I mean. In his heart of hearts, I think he'd still love to see me step right into his shoes, and run the day-to-day business at the office, as well, but he seems more willing to compromise now than he's ever been."

"Being so sick has changed him," she said softly.

"It has," he agreed soberly. "And, well, I guess seeing him this way has changed me, too. We're both a little less stubborn than we used to be."

"Connor, I'm so glad. This has been hard for both of you."

"Well, it's not time to break out the champagne just yet." He gave her an echo of a smile. "We haven't dotted all the i's, by any means. But we came to a general agreement that when the time came, when he's forced to give up his interest in Triple I, I'll be willing to have some say in running the company."

He gave a sigh that was pure relief, and Maggie smiled back at him. They both knew what he really meant—that Kincaid wasn't expected to live much longer, and that Connor's involvement in the company would be tied to his father's death. It wasn't an easy thing to deal with.

"And that's enough business for now," he pronounced, and managed to recapture her in his arms. "More to the point..."

It took him a while to get to the point, because he found himself distracted all over again by that little pout to Maggie's lower lip, and the way it seemed to invite him to kiss it. And he could never stop there, because the sweet scent of her skin acted on him like a heady wine, and he had to go on tasting her, letting his lips explore the creamy softness of her neck and collarbone.

"You're driving me crazy, Maggie Lewis," he murmured against her cheek. "Can't we get together alone, without a chaperon for a change?" He buried his face in her sweet-smelling hair, reveling in the subtle perfume that was pure Maggie.

"Jordan is going away next weekend," she whispered, and Connor felt his heart leap in anticipation. "I could come and visit you then."

"When?" He had to pin her down, make it certain.

"When will you be free?"

"I'll be done with work about seven on Saturday morning."

"Won't you be exhausted by then?"

"Come and see me, and find out."

"All right," she agreed, smiling.

He heard a car in the driveway; that was probably their pizza. Before releasing Maggie, he looked into her eyes for a few more moments and saw a new possibility there, as though they'd put their troubles behind them and the future held only good things. How could anything go wrong now, Connor wondered, when they wanted each other this fiercely?

Seven

By Friday the spring storm had blown itself out, and Saturday morning was sunny and pristine, washed by several days of April showers. Connor's building was in a part of Boston that Maggie wouldn't have wanted to travel to at night, but at 7:00 a.m. on a Saturday morning the area was all but deserted, and the bright sunshine made it look more attractive than the old industrial buildings had any right to be.

She'd already rung his doorbell and gotten no answer. There was no sign of his van, either, and she'd settled herself back into her car to wait for him. It was so easy to picture him, in his navy sweater and old brown leather jacket. The dark colors always made the flash of his teeth, when he grinned, seem even whiter, and Maggie smiled to herself just thinking about him.

Connor's gentle tap on her car window made her jump a little. As she stepped out of the car and into his one-armed

embrace, she smiled to see that his other hand was occupied holding onto a pile of packages wrapped in foil.

"Breakfast?" she asked him.

"Of a sort."

"Does your engine block cook omelets?"

"Not very well. They tend to come out like last year's
shoe leather." They were walking into the building now,
arms around each other. "The same goes for soufflés, I'm
afraid. So I hope you don't mind eating chicken breasts with
asparagus stuffing for breakfast."

"It sounds wonderful."

Maggie wasn't surprised to find that Connor's apartment was about as different from the Blakes' comfortable
Wellesley home as it was possible to be. The big, open space
had clearly once been part of a factory floor. A couple of
walls had been added, screening what Maggie assumed was
the bedroom. A well-equipped kitchen occupied one end of
the apartment. Clearly Connor didn't do all his cooking on
his engine block, Maggie thought with a smile. A long
workbench took up another wall, and a few comfortable
chairs and a sofa made a living area in front of the broad
expanse of windows.

The windows faced south, and the still-rising run was
flooding the place with light. "That's how I feel," Maggie
murmured, as Connor set their breakfast down on his
workbench and recaptured her in his arms. "Just spilling
over with sunlight."

"I take it you're not just making small talk about the
weather," Connor growled against her hair, and Maggie
smiled and shook her head.

She was beginning to be caught up in the familiar excitement of being close to him, with the added spark of knowledge that now she could live out the fantasies he'd inspired
from the very beginning. Her face was close to his chest, and
by the sound of his heartbeat steadily picking up speed, she
guessed some very similar fantasies were racing through his
mind, too.

"I've got some champagne chilling in the refrigerator," he said, "but maybe we should leave it there a while longer."

"Champagne and chicken breasts first thing in the morning," Maggie mused, with a smile. "When you change things around, you really do it with a vengeance, don't you?"

His smoldering, dark eyes told her that wasn't all he did with a vengeance. The hunger in his face was almost a physical force. "Of course," he said. "And it isn't first thing in the morning, anyway. This is the end of a hard day's work."

"Are you sure you wouldn't rather just go to bed and have a good night's sleep?" She knew her eyes were dancing now, locked with his and exchanging a good deal more than words ever could.

"I'd rather go to bed, all right," he said huskily. "But sleep can wait."

Impatiently he shrugged out of his leather jacket, letting it drop beside their breakfast on the end of the workbench. Maggie drew in a deep breath, astonished all over again by his rugged male beauty, and the powerful, masculine shape of his upper body.

For years now she'd been restraining her own natural boldness, reining in the impulses that had made her such a hellion in her childhood. But Connor set those deeply buried feelings free again, and she felt herself gratefully letting go of all those carefully learned, polite rules for a well-trained young woman.

She couldn't wait to feel all of him, and as soon as he'd shed his coat and turned to her again, she ran her hands along the taut skin at his waist, sliding her fingers beneath the hem of his navy sweater. His muffled groan told her how much he liked that, and she continued upward, exploring the muscled planes of his chest and delighting in the springiness of the hairs sprinkling his broad torso.

She could picture those fine black hairs, and suddenly she wanted to see all of him, to be completely wrapped up with him without the barrier of clothing. As if he sensed her thoughts, he pulled the sweater over his head. His body was more imposing than she'd imagined, with his strength showing plainly in the smooth muscles of his shoulders, and his flat stomach dusted with that jet-black hair that led her eyes inexorably lower, to the waistband of his worn blue jeans.

"Connor..." Her voice came out breathy with wonder and desire.

"Tell me I'm not dreaming, Maggie. I've been thinking of this for so long." His words ended in another groan, as she ran her hands over his skin.

"I'm not sure *I'm* not dreaming," she told him. "But I don't really care."

"That's the spirit." His grin managed to break through the clouded passion on his face. Then his own impatience seemed to get the better of him, and he suddenly lifted her off the floor and held her against his chest. "If this is a dream, I'm all for it," he said, and strode into the walled-off bedroom.

Maggie half remembered standing in front of her closet at six that morning, carefully deciding what to wear. She'd finally chosen a pair of comfortable jeans and a pale lavender cotton cardigan, but all the care that had gone into the decision seemed silly now, when her only desire was to be out of the clothes that kept her from feeling Connor's skin against her own.

The bedroom was small and intimate. The bed took up most of the floor space, and after the first few seconds Maggie was unaware of her surroundings anyway. All that mattered was Connor, leaning on one elbow at her side and expertly undoing the small ivory buttons at the front of her sweater.

She was humming with desire, aching to know the touch of his hands on her skin. As she pulled the sweater free and undid the clasp of her lacy bra, she was already lost in the sensations of his breath and his fingers discovering the

softest, smoothest parts of her. Pushing her jeans and panties into a pile on the floor took only seconds.

"Maggie." The open adoration in his voice shook her.
"You're so lovely, even lovelier than I knew you would be."

She could sense him controlling the fury of his need for
her, forcing himself to take things slowly. He lowered his
dark head and kissed her collarbone, making her aware of
every nerve ending from one shoulder to the other. She
couldn't bear to close her eyes; the sight of Connor's lips
grazing her white skin was too enticing. Wordlessly she
watched as he moved lower, planting small kisses on her
flesh. He circled the full roundness of her breast with his
hand, and covered its taut center with his warm, searching
mouth.

Maggie couldn't keep silent any longer. Her cry of pleasure shot straight through her, and the throbbing need inside threatened to spill over as Connor expertly teased and
aroused her. For what seemed like forever, his tongue gave
her an unimaginable pleasure with its sweeping movements
across her hardened nipple. She cried out again and again,
begging him to satisfy the longings he was conjuring up.

He was maddeningly slow about answering her plea. He
turned his face into the warm hollow between her breasts,
and murmured indistinctly, "If the people who make per-
fumes knew how good you smell, they'd give up in despair." His fingers glanced over her skin, light as butterflies
but always knowing exactly what would please her most,
what would make her pulse race and her voice gasp out his
name on that note of longing.

"Please, Connor," she said, arching her whole body as
his hands found the sweet, pulsating center of her. "Please,
I need to feel you inside me."

"And you will." *But not yet*, his roughened tone seemed
to say. First he was bent on arousing her to the point of de-
lirium, as his touch sent her imagination spiraling off into
outer space. At the same time, she'd never been more aware
of her own body, and every small shift in Connor's touch

seemed to set off a chain reaction of new pleasures deep inside.

She was trembling on the brink of ecstasy, with nothing holding her back but the need to be completely possessed by him. "Oh, God, Connor..." Something in her voice as she said his name must have communicated that overwhelming need to him, because suddenly his self-control seemed to give way.

"Now," she gasped.

"Now," he echoed, the word forcing its way past his clenched teeth. He rid himself of his blue jeans, and leaned over Maggie on the bed, propping himself on his elbows as he looked deeply into her eyes. The feeling of having his lean, hard body covering her was driving her crazy, and she moved her legs against his, delighting in the sensations that raced through her.

The pressure of his own need was unmistakable, and Maggie surprised herself with her own boldness in caressing him, bringing him the same intense pleasure, the way he'd just done for her. She was far past any kind of rational thought now. All that mattered was this surpassing hunger for each other. The primitive rhythm of it was beginning to take over both their movements, and Maggie abandoned herself to it willingly.

Connor shifted himself until he was poised above Maggie, and one look into her face seemed to satisfy him that she was more than ready for him. His first thrust filled her completely, and Maggie heard his low groan mingled with her own cry of wonder. Once again she could sense him trying to rein in his escalating passion, but she couldn't keep herself from moving against him, urging them both on to the sweet fulfillment she seemed to have been waiting for all her life.

They were completely united now, their motions dictated by a force inside both of them. Maggie felt a lifetime's worth of fetters falling away, just as Connor's dark eyes had promised her they would, that first night she'd seen him. He moved deeper into her, holding her in a powerful embrace that she answered gladly. She wrapped herself around him, welcoming him inside her with each convulsive thrust. Behind her closed eyelids, images swam and dissolved like magic, but she knew the true magic was the one they were reaching for together.

His grip tightened, and Maggie heard herself cry out just before the wave of sensation swept her away. He took her higher and higher, and cried out himself as they reached the trembling peak together and hovered there, holding on to that moment of pure, distilled pleasure as long as they could.

Maggie was left gasping, all the breath dragged out of her by that fierce undertow. She clung to him without speaking, even when he finally shifted his weight and moved to lie beside her on the bed.

"I've been waiting for you all my life," he whispered, and she nodded silently.

It was a long while before he spoke again, and when he did, his voice sounded sleepy and distant. "Ready for champagne?" he said.

Maggie was surprised by her own drowsiness. She'd had a busy week, and thoughts of Connor had kept her from sleeping well. Now that she was locked in his arms, all the tension was draining out of her body.

"Maybe in a minute," she replied lazily, and half-opened her eyes to look at him. He was smiling, with his eyes closed, and Maggie reached down to pull up the blanket at the bottom of the bed. "Good night, Connor," she murmured, and snuggled herself back against the warmth of his body.

She was completely disoriented when she woke up. Worse yet, she was alone, although after a few seconds she identified noises coming from the kitchen. Hastily dressing herself in her jeans and lavender cardigan again, she followed the sounds and found Connor in the act of putting the chicken breasts, still wrapped in foil, into the oven.

"I thought you might be taking them out for a drive," she teased, coming up behind him. "Just to warm them up again."

"I do cook in the kitchen some of the time," he replied, closing the oven door and turning to take her in his arms. He was dressed again, too, in jeans and an old blue sweatshirt that did nothing to hide the powerful muscles of his upper body. Making love hadn't been nearly the permanent cure she'd expected, Maggie thought wonderingly, as she felt the heat of desire for him suffusing her whole body again.

"What time is it?" she asked. "I've completely lost track."

"It's about noon."

"We've been sleeping for four hours?"

"Yep. You must have needed a nap."

"Four hours is a pretty long nap," she said. "And a pretty short night's sleep, if that's what it was for you. Aren't you tired?"

"Wonderfully tired." He grinned broadly, and kissed her. The grin made the fatigue in his face seem less pronounced, and the kiss made her forget about everything except the feeling of being close to him. "*Now* are you ready for champagne?"

"Serve it up." Since everything had already been turned on its head anyway, Maggie determined to do things with a vengeance, the way Connor did. Champagne at noon—or was it the middle of the night?—seemed perfectly appropriate.

The chicken was warm again by the time they were on their second glass of champagne, and Maggie tossed together a salad from some lettuce and vegetables that Connor had in his refrigerator. She thought it was one of the best meals she'd ever had.

"Maybe I'm wasting my talents," Connor said, helping himself to more salad. "I should probably open a restaurant instead."

"Connor's Engine-block Cookery," Maggie suggested.

"That has a nice ring to it. Maybe it should be a catering company, not a restaurant. I could heat things up on the way to the party."

"And chill the champagne in the back of the van," Maggie said, laughing. "You'd make a fortune."

Connor shook his head. "Nobody makes a fortune in the food business, as far as I can tell," he said. "And I grew up with a fortune, anyway. I'd much rather work for the love of it, not just to make money."

"You really love your job, don't you?"

He shrugged. "To be honest, there are parts of it that don't appeal to me all that much any more."

"Which parts are those?"

"Well, a lot of the calls I get are pretty depressing. You know, people who've been robbed, like you were."

"I didn't realize you thought our meeting was depressing," Maggie teased.

"Not at all," he replied smoothly. "As a matter of fact, our meeting was what made me realize just how depressing some of my other calls really are. I get a lot of work through the police department, and I see a lot of domestic disputes. And I'm not as crazy as I used to be about the idea of working all night. Four in the morning loses its charm after a few years."

"I can believe that." Maggie studied him for a moment. The strong, masculine lines of his face and the laughter in his eyes made him more appealing than any man she'd ever known. "What would you do for a living, if you could do anything you wanted?" she asked him suddenly.

He answered without hesitation. "I'd set myself up making the alarm systems I've designed," he said, nodding his dark head toward the workbench on the far wall. It was covered with what looked like rolled-up plans and unidentifiable electronic devices. "It's something I know I'm good at, and there's always a market for a good security system."

"You should do it, then," Maggie said. "Start your own company, I mean."

He shook his head again, and smiled. "That takes a lot of capital," he said. "More than I've got, even as a member of the Blake family. And I'm good at designing the things, but I'm not sure I'd be any good at all at manufacturing them or marketing them. Maybe I'll sell the idea to somebody someday. Beyond that, it's just a pipe dream, I'm afraid."

"Sounds like you could use some investment counseling from Triple I." She'd meant the words as a joke, but as soon as she'd said them, she could see that the mention of the family firm was something Connor still couldn't joke about. His face clouded over.

"I tried to figure out the investment world," he told her seriously, "and it was slightly less comprehensible to me than Greek. My father is thrilled that I'm considering having something to do with Triple I again, but I'm beginning to wonder whether it isn't the stupidest business decision he ever made."

"Your father may have his blind spots," Maggie said, "but I never heard anyone accuse him of making stupid business decisions. And I think we should declare a holiday from business talk, anyway. I'm sorry I brought the subject up." She edged her chair closer to Connor's. "What's on your agenda for the rest of today?"

Slowly, the familiar roguish gleam came back into his eyes, and she knew she'd succeeded in thoroughly changing the subject.

"Nothing specific," he said, "but now that I've had my good night's sleep, I thought maybe I'd have the strength to sweep you off your feet again. How does that sound?"

"Like an offer I can't refuse," Maggie said, and she knew her own eyes were gleaming in reply. She rose to meet him as he moved to take her in his arms, and with a smile of renewed pleasure at his touch, she filed the subject of their future away to be dealt with later.

* * *

Maggie couldn't decide whether the day seemed long or short, busy or lazy. It was as though she'd stepped through the looking glass when she'd entered Connor's apartment early that morning, and time seemed to be acting very strangely.

Making love with Connor was a revelation each time. Late that night, as they settled down in front of the television to watch the late movie, she confided almost shyly, "You make me feel things I've never felt before."

Connor looked down into her face. "The same goes for me," he said gravely. "And somehow I knew from the first moment I saw you—even before I knew who you were—that you would make me feel this way."

He drew his hand over the smooth curve of her breast, and Maggie shivered in response. "It's not fair, the things you do to me," she murmured. They'd had dinner at ten o'clock, normally Maggie's bedtime, and she'd gotten her second wind with a vengeance. She felt as though she could stay awake all night. "Are you taking the night off?" she asked him, remembering that he usually worked on Saturday nights.

"More or less," he replied, settling his arm around Maggie's shoulders on his aged but comfortable sofa. "I told my answering service only to forward calls that were absolute emergencies."

"Then I'll keep my fingers crossed that there aren't any of those," Maggie said.

She didn't cross them quite hard enough, as it turned out. They were halfway into a movie when the phone rang. Maggie glanced at her watch as Connor went to answer it; it was almost one in the morning.

She could hear Connor speaking over the sound of the television set. "Is this something that could possibly wait until tomorrow? No, I see. You're right, it does sound necessary. All right, I'll be there in half an hour."

He hung up, and came back to sit beside Maggie. "Sorry," he said, kissing her hair. "Duty calls. I shouldn't be long."

Maggie switched off the set. "I'm coming with you," she told him.

"There's no need for that. It's just a simple matter of changing a lock. Shouldn't take more than an hour."

"I'd rather be with you."

"Don't you want to see how the movie ends?"

"I suspect they end up living happily ever after. That's good enough for me."

"Okay," he said. "Grab your coat. I should warn you, though, this isn't going to be a very scenic expedition."

In the van, he explained what he'd meant. "The call was from a woman in Roxbury," he said. "She'd just thrown her husband out of their apartment—I'll spare you the list of names she called him first—and she's afraid he's going to come back and beat her up. Apparently he's done it before. She's going to try to get a restraining order, but in the meantime the police have told her the smartest thing to do is to get the locks changed."

"It sounds pretty grim," Maggie commented.

"But not all that uncommon, unfortunately."

Connor was steering the van through parts of Boston that were a far cry from the neat, tree-lined streets of Wellesley. "This brings back memories," Maggie said, as they passed rows of houses whose paint had long since peeled off. "I grew up in a neighborhood like this one."

"Until you moved to a rich woman's house in Westchester County," Connor speculated. "Must have been quite a leap."

"Oh, it was." Maggie smiled, only half amused. "Maybe too much of a leap. There are still times when I feel like an impostor in Wellesley."

Connor gave her a sharp look, but didn't reply. Checking the address he'd written on a scrap of paper, he turned the van onto a cul-de-sac littered with rubbish, and turned off the engine. "I'd feel better if you waited here," he said, climbing into the back of the van in search of the tools he needed. "This won't take long."

Maggie didn't mind staying in the van. This reminder of her old neighborhood was unexpectedly depressing, and when a thin-faced woman answered Connor's ring Maggie was unsettled by the obvious fear on her face. She remembered that feeling so well: fear of the authorities, fear of the landlord, fear of someone bigger than you, fear of being caught stealing something. She'd come a long way since her childhood in Newark, but never far enough to forget the fear and despair that poverty could bring.

She was dealing with her own unpleasant memories when a rusty car drove up and parked behind Connor's van. A big man got out of it. He walked unsteadily but belligerently, like someone who was drunk enough to want to pick a fight. It made Maggie uneasy, especially when the man headed up the sidewalk toward the house where Connor was working.

She hesitated for a moment, and then turned around to survey the tools in the back of the van. Most of them were small, but there was one large wrench that looked as if it would make a passable weapon. Grabbing it in one hand, Maggie swung down from the passenger seat and headed for the house.

She could hear Connor's voice as she stepped into the dimly lit hallway. She could tell he was trying to sound calm and reasonable, countering the threat in the other man's voice.

"I'm telling you it's my damn apartment, and you'd better let me in there or you'll be sorry," the big man was saying loudly enough for everyone in the building to hear.

"Sorry, buddy," Connor replied evenly. "I've got a job to do here."

Maggie reached the top of the first flight of stairs, and saw Connor taking the cylinder out of a door lock. His face was in shadow, but the hall light illuminated the other man's features, and the violence Maggie saw there made her stomach tighten into a knot.

"Maureen!" The man raised his voice to a shout, and he banged a fist on the door Connor was working on. "Maureen, you get out here! You can't do this to me."

Hurry, Connor, Maggie pleaded silently. Almost placidly, he started installing a new cylinder, as though the big man looming over him didn't exist.

"This is your fault, pal," the man said. "That's my wife in there, and I got a right to go in."

"Well, the police seem to think she has a right to keep you out if she wants to," Connor said. He sounded calm enough, but Maggie could see by the glint in his dark eyes that the man was rubbing him the wrong way.

"Yeah, the police love sticking their noses in other people's business, don't they? Maureen, I'm giving you about two seconds to get out here."

He kicked the door viciously, and Connor looked up. "Would you mind not doing that?" he said. "Makes it hard to work."

For a moment the man seemed confused, and Connor was able to finish installing the new lock. But when he tapped gently on the door and said, "Mrs. Babbit, I'm going to slide the new keys under the door, all right?" the husband lost what was left of his temper.

"The hell you will!" he yelled. "Locking me out of my own place."

Maggie took in a deep breath as the man wound up and let fly at Connor with a sloppy but powerful punch. Connor was caught off balance, half standing in front of the lock he'd just installed, and the blow knocked him against the wall with a force that Maggie could feel from several feet away.

"Stop it!" she shouted, and ran the rest of the way up the stairs to the landing. She held up the heavy wrench in her hand.

Connor was getting to his feet, wincing. "Maggie, get out of here," he said. "I can handle it."

"Oh, yeah?" The man glared at both of them, enraged to the point of recklessness. "Well, handle this, Superman!"

He swung again, and Connor dodged, letting the man's fist connect with the crumbling plaster on the wall. He gave an angry bellow, like a bull moose on the rampage, and got ready to take another shot.

Connor was too quick for him, landing a neat right to the jaw. But as soon as he'd moved, Maggie saw the pain in his face, as though something was wrong with his right shoulder. She remembered that bone-cracking jolt when he'd been knocked against the wall, and knew he'd been hurt.

"That's enough!" she said, stepping quickly between the two men. A blast of stale beer on the husband's breath filled her nostrils, and she caught a glimpse of his wife's frightened face peering out of a crack in the door.

"Well, this seems to be the ladies' night for ordering people around, doesn't it?" the man leered.

Maggie hefted the wrench, feeling her own temper starting to go. "Well, I've got the same order for you that your wife does," she told him. "Get out of here, and make it snappy."

Something in her face seemed to stop him, and she hoped desperately that he was mostly bark and not much bite. "Pushy, aren't you?" he said.

"You bet I am." She could sense Connor right behind her, holding his injured shoulder and waiting, as she was, to see which way the man would turn.

"Well, that's too bad." He reached out and grabbed the door handle, and then yelped in pain when Maggie brought the wrench down hard on his wrist. "Why, you—"

Maggie didn't give him a chance to call her names. All her fighting instincts were coming to the surface, and she astonished herself by dredging up words she hadn't even thought of for fifteen years. She started with "bully" and worked her way through a list of epithets called up from the street-fighting days of her youth, and by the time she was done with him, the formidable Mr. Babbit was backing down the stairs as though he couldn't wait to get away from her.

"All right, all right, for crying out loud," he was whining, clearly trying to leave with what dignity he could. "I'll be back, Maureen. Don't forget that."

The outer door slammed behind him, and Maggie turned slowly to see Connor looking at her with mixed wonder and amusement. "Now I understand the meaning of the phrase 'tongue-lashing,'" he said, with a faint grin.

"Connor, are you all right? Your shoulder—"

"I'll survive." The grin faded as he tried to move his shoulder. Maggie could tell how much it hurt him.

The apartment door opened slowly, and Maureen's thin face looked out at them. "I'm sorry," she said. "I thought you'd be done by the time he came back."

"It's all right, Mrs. Babbit. After some of the things Maggie said to him, I don't think you'll have to worry about seeing him again any time soon."

The woman was still too frightened to smile. "I always knew he'd back down if a woman stood up to him," she said to Maggie. "I just never had the courage to do it."

Maggie waited while Mrs. Babbit paid Connor's bill—in cash—and then preceded Connor down the stairs. "It wasn't anything like courage," she said wryly, opening the outer door and breathing the comparatively fresh air gratefully. "It was just years of training."

"Well, one thing's certain," Connor replied, painfully hoisting his toolbox into the van. "I'll never call you a proper Wellesley lady again."

Despite Connor's protests, Maggie insisted on driving the van. "You don't look like you're in any shape to be shifting gears," she told him, climbing into the driver's seat and adjusting it for her shorter legs.

And she overrode his objections again when he saw that she was heading not for his apartment but for Boston City Hospital.

"That shoulder could be dislocated or broken," she told him.

"It's probably just bruised," he grunted, as he got out of the van in front of the emergency entrance. "Boston City's used to getting stab and bullet wounds. They're going to think it's pretty funny to see a guy with a bruise on his shoulder."

As it happened, no one laughed at Connor's shoulder, which turned out to be badly sprained. "It's been my Achilles' heel for years," he explained to Maggie, as the emergency-room doctor taped him up. "I hurt it at college."

"Playing football?"

"No, throwing the javelin. I never was much for team sports. I preferred the ones where they let you make your own decisions."

They were both thoughtful as they got back into the van. Maggie wondered if he was thinking the same thing she was: that in coming to a compromise with his father, Connor was going to have to be part of a team whether he liked it or not. She tried to picture him at the biweekly Triple I board meetings she'd been attending for five years now. It wasn't an easy picture. Triple I, with its set policies and conservative outlook on things in general, was the last place in the world Connor Blake seemed to fit.

"Getting sleepy yet?" he asked, turning the lights back on in his apartment.

"It's funny, but I'm not. Maybe it's just the novelty of being up while most of the city is asleep. You look tired, though, Connor. Does your shoulder hurt very much?"

He walked stiffly into the kitchen area and took down a bottle from one of the cupboards. "Some," he said tersely.

Maggie reached into her purse. "Do you want some of the painkillers they gave you at the hospital?"

"No, thanks. Those things always make me groggy. Anyway," he gave her a faint grin, "liquor is quicker. Can I pour you a drink?"

"Just a small one." She accepted the glass of brandy he held out to her, and sipped it slowly. Connor drained his at one swallow, and poured another.

"What would it take to entice you into accompanying the poor invalid back to bed?" he asked, his grin wider now.

It didn't take much enticing, at all. Maggie went with him gladly, leaving her glass on the bedside table and laying down beside him when he stretched himself full-length on the bed. She could feel the excitement building in her all over again, at the nearness of his magnificent body and the invitation in his dark brown eyes.

"If the phone rings again, I'm planning to ignore it," told her. The way he was watching her made her blood race.

"Good plan," she said, and moved closer to him, lowering her mouth until it met his. He tasted so good, his masculine scent mingling with the slight aftertaste of brandy. His tongue swept over hers in seductive circles until she quivered all over, longing to make love with him again.

"I'm afraid I'm not capable of anything very athletic," he said, when she finally raised her head.

Maggie ran a gentle hand over his injured shoulder, and smiled. Suddenly she felt bolder than she'd ever been, so certain of the attraction between them that she had no thoughts of anything but the pleasure they could bring each other. "Good," she said, "because all you need to do is stay right where you are."

She saw him raise his eyebrows in surprise, and then lift them even further as he understood what she was saying. Still smiling, she pulled his worn blue sweatshirt over his head, gently disentangling it from his right arm. The hard muscles of his chest excited her, making her want to explore all of him with her hands and lips.

"God, Maggie, if you only knew what that does to me," he groaned, as she ran her hands over his skin. The feeling of the jet black hairs on his chest was like an answering caress, and she followed the line of them downward until she heard his groan deepen. She undid the zipper of his jeans without haste, wanting to make this last, wanting to savor the desire she was feeling in every part of her.

She couldn't do that fully with her own clothing in the way. She was conscious of his burning gaze as she shed her sweater and jeans, and the hunger in his eyes was as arousing as if he'd been touching her. When she lay back down against the length of his body, she was achingly aware of his arousal, and the need to feel him inside her began to dominate all her other thoughts.

She drew in a deep breath, and slid herself over him, reveling in the thousand sensations of her smooth flesh against his thighs. Connor's eyes were closed, and Maggie reached up to smooth his hair back from his forehead. She had never dreamed she could take such pleasure from touching a man, or from kissing his closed eyelids and hearing him say her name in a low voice that was half a whisper and half an entreaty.

Slowly, lovingly, Maggie's caresses moved downward. His skin was so firm and alive, stretched taut over the hard planes of his chest. She turned her face to the sprinkling of dark hair across his stomach, and delighted in the sense of his strength beneath her. Her hands outlined his lean hips and powerful thighs, finally reaching the place where he throbbed and burned with an overwhelming need for her. She could tell minutely how her movements inflamed him, and when she moved lower still to surround him with the moist warmth of her mouth, his hoarse cry had a note in it that was very close to agony.

She'd meant this to be slow and endless, but the feel of him, and the sound of his voice calling her name, excited her beyond any rational thoughts of pacing or plans. The ache inside her reminded her insistently of a place that only Connor had ever discovered or satisfied.

She moved over him, and in one long thrust he buried himself inside her. She held herself perfectly still for a long moment, luxuriating in the tremors that ran through her, and then she began to move, slowly at first, but she was caught up immediately in the pulsating rhythm that their mutual desire created.

It was impossible to control what that rhythm dictated. Maggie let herself be swept along in it, barely aware of Connor's hands fiercely gripping her arms, outlining her form, or of her voice calling his name. They were in headlong pursuit of the same shimmering place in the distance, which Maggie had seen beckoning to her in Connor's eyes since the first night she'd met him. They moved together as one person, driven by the same need.

They reached that beckoning place together, so explosively that Maggie felt suspended in time. It took several shuddering minutes for the real world to come back into focus again. When it finally did, she saw by the look on Connor's face that he was as astonished and fulfilled as she had been.

"Not bad for an invalid," she said, when she could trust her voice again.

He grinned, almost languidly. "We invalids know enough to let the lady do all the work," he replied. In spite of their lighthearted words, both of them were still lost in a sense of wonder at the experience they'd just shared.

When Connor reached over to turn out the bedside lamp, Maggie thought to ask sleepily, "Is it night or day out?"

"I've lost track."

"So have I." She eased herself against him under the covers, carefully avoiding his shoulder. "It's funny. It doesn't seem to matter any more, does it?"

Eight

─────

Time continued to be of no importance until late Sunday afternoon, when Maggie regretfully announced that she'd promised to pick Jordan up at five o'clock.

"They've been on a school trip to New York," she said. "The bus is supposed to have them back to the school by five."

"Things sure have changed at The Stearns School," Connor said. "When I was there, we were lucky if we got to go as far as the Museum of Fine Arts in Boston."

"Somehow I still have trouble picturing you as a proper young Stearns boy," Maggie told him. She saw the flash of his white teeth as he smiled.

"Not so proper," he said. "When we *did* get to the Museum, I managed to skip out of the Impressionist gallery and spend the afternoon outside exploring the Back Bay fens instead."

"Now *that* I can picture, with no trouble at all!" Maggie laughed. "Anyway, I hate to say it, but I should be going."

Connor found himself suddenly at a loss for words, staring down into those gold-and-hazel eyes that were more magical than ever. They'd managed to avoid the subject of what the future held for them after this weekend, as though neither of them had wanted to break the spell. But now he wanted to make this real, to make sure Maggie Lewis wasn't going to vanish back into her safe, secure world and leave him alone again.

He was still trying to put his thoughts into words when the phone in his kitchen rang. "Duty calls?" Maggie suggested, raising her eyebrows in a gesture that made her even more bewitching.

"It had better not," he replied. "Don't go just yet, Maggie. I'll try to make this quick."

Standing in the hallway, Maggie watched him through the open apartment door. All of yesterday's weariness had left his face by now, and he was looking positively boyish today in blue jeans and a well-worn red T-shirt that said "K.C.'s All-Night Locksmith" across the back. His shoulder looked only slightly stiff as he reached for the ringing phone.

Things are finally sorting themselves out, Maggie thought. *Aren't they?* For some reason, she had a nagging sense that in spite of the wonder and the passion of their weekend together, there were still questions to be answered before she and Connor could fully share each other's lives.

Maybe she was getting psychic, or maybe she'd known that this phone call would come sooner or later, and overturn the delicate balance she and Connor had managed to reach. She couldn't hear his words, but from the tone of his voice she guessed that he was speaking to his mother. And from the look on his face, she knew the news wasn't good.

"I see. Yes, I understand." His words were clipped and serious. "I'll be right over. Wait till I get there. I'll drive you to the hospital."

When he hung up, his boyish mood was long gone. He grabbed his old leather jacket from the coatrack, and turned to face Maggie. "That was my mother," he said. "They just took my father to the hospital in an ambulance."

"His heart?" Maggie asked. She knew from Connor's face that it must be serious.

"Yes, and it doesn't sound good. My mother doesn't trust herself to drive. She sounds pretty shaken up, so I'm going to take her to the hospital. She says," he added, with a bitterly amused smile, "that at a time like this, she doesn't feel right turning to the servants for help. So much for all the good things money can buy you."

Maggie wasn't sure what to say. She could imagine all the feelings churning up inside Connor at the thought that his father might be dying, and she knew now wasn't the time to try to deal with them. "I'll go and collect Jordan at the school," she said. "And then I'll meet you at the hospital, if you want me to."

"Yes." His blunt answer reassured her that he really did want her to be there. "They've taken him to Brigham and Women's. That's where his doctor is. And Maggie?"

They were both standing in the doorway now, and in spite of the urgency of the moment, Maggie could feel that ever-present magnetism flickering between them. "Yes?" she said softly, putting her hands up to rest on his shoulders. The worn leather was rough under her fingertips, in contrast to the smooth muscles of Connor's neck.

"In case things get crazy and there isn't time for us to talk, just remember—you and I have a future to discuss, and I don't intend to let you forget it."

"I won't forget it." She whispered the words, answering the promise in Connor's dark eyes. He lowered his head to kiss her lips, and Maggie could feel her body responding to him in a persistent echo of the passion they'd shared that weekend.

Then he said a hasty goodbye, and almost raced her down the stairs to the parking lot. His van was screeching out of the lot by the time she'd unlocked her car and turned the key in the ignition.

* * *

The phone was ringing when Maggie arrived at her house with Jordan. "Could you get that, honey?" she asked him, starting up the broad staircase. "I've got to get changed."

Her plan was to call Caroline Lewis, and see whether either Caroline or Bobbie could watch Jordan that evening while Maggie went to the hospital. But word had traveled fast, it seemed, and she was only half-changed into a skirt and sweater when Jordan called up the stairs that his grandmother was on the phone and wanted to speak to Maggie.

"Hello, Caroline," she said, picking up the bedroom extension as she twisted her body to do up the buttons on her skirt.

"Maggie, have you heard about Kincaid?"

"Yes, as a matter of fact, I was just on my way to the hospital to see how he's doing. Do you want to come along?"

"If you can manage it. Maria just called me to tell me. She said it didn't look very, well, very hopeful. Why don't you drop Jordan off here? Bobbie can keep an eye on him."

"I'll be right over," Maggie promised. Connor might make off-the-cuff remarks about the old family network, she thought fleetingly, but she had to admit it was pretty efficient when it came to rallying around.

Traffic was unexpectedly heavy. Everyone seemed to have gone out of the city for the warm spring weekend, and Maggie had to battle the returning hordes to reach the hospital. "I hope Connor didn't get held up like this," she said, as they sat in a long line at a traffic light.

Caroline Lewis shot her one of those shrewdly penetrating looks that had always seemed out of place with her serene, elegant image. Maggie had learned in the past eight years never to underestimate her mother-in-law. "He's driving his mother to the hospital, is he?" was all she said.

"Yes." Maggie wondered how much those shrewd blue eyes had already figured out about her budding relationship with Connor. "I—I was with him when his mother called with the news."

"I see." Caroline nodded thoughtfully. "We did wonder, Maria and I, how you managed to effect a truce between Connor and his father last weekend. Now I think I understand." Her brief smile showed how much she approved of the idea.

The light finally changed and Maggie put her foot down on the accelerator, willing the traffic to disappear. It felt like hours since she had left Connor's apartment. Had it taken him this long to reach the hospital? She ached for him, knowing what he must be feeling.

She dropped Caroline at the entrance, and went to find a parking space. By the time she'd left the car and hurried to the front desk, she was out of breath. But there was no need for her to ask what floor Kincaid was on, and to go racing up there. Caroline was waiting for her, and a glance at her mother-in-law's face told Maggie all she needed to know.

"They couldn't save him," Caroline confirmed sadly. "It was what they'd predicted for some time—his heart just wasn't strong enough to stand another attack. Maria asked me to come down and wait for Jacquie and Richard. They're on their way now. I can give you the room number, if you want to go up."

"I think I do," Maggie said, and followed Caroline's directions. But when she reached the room, she couldn't bring herself to go in. Connor and his mother stood by the bedside, almost lost in the shadows. Someone had closed the curtains, Maggie thought, and she decided not to intrude on what was a very private moment of grief. She slipped away from the door, and rejoined Caroline downstairs.

When Jacquie and Richard arrived, all of them went to Kincaid's room together, and Maggie found herself just one more face in the small crowd. Now was not the time for anything personal between her and Connor. This was a family gathering, and she was nothing more than a member of the Lewis family, at the moment. She reminded herself of Connor's promise that the two of them had a future to discuss. The time to discuss it would come before long, she told herself.

The next week was a difficult one for Maggie. She saw a great deal of Connor—at his home, at the funeral parlor, at the funeral itself, and the gathering for family and friends after the memorial service the next Sunday. But there was no chance to speak to him alone, or to know just what he was feeling. It was hard to be close to him, and to see the new seriousness in his face accentuated by the somber, dark gray suit he must have found time to buy, without being able to touch him, or share his thoughts.

Their one private moment together came in the midst of the large gathering at the Blakes' house after the memorial service. Maggie was circulating around the room, visiting with people she knew while keeping half an eye on Jordan and his young cousins, in case they forgot that this was a serious gathering and started having too noisy a reunion. At the table where punch and refreshments were being served, she stopped to refill her glass, and found herself only a few feet from Connor and a man she didn't recognize. Something about him made Maggie class him as a businessman.

"That's good news, K.C.," the man was saying. Maggie saw Connor wince slightly at the use of the family nickname. "We've been wondering when Triple I was going to join the rest of us in the twentieth century."

"I guess it had to happen sooner or later," Connor smiled.

"It's too bad your father didn't see it that way. I hear you've been beating the bushes for new recruits already. You don't waste any time, do you?"

"I always did like to get things rolling in a hurry. I haven't signed up anyone new yet, of course. I'll have to get the board's approval first, but I've been doing a lot of research, the past few days."

"Well, good for you. Let me know when you're ready to roll."

"Thanks, I will. Keep it under your hat just for now, though, will you? I'm not saying it's a definite thing yet, just that it's the direction I'd like to see things go."

"Well, you'll have a lot of support, in that case."

"*And* a lot of opposition." For an instant Connor showed a trace of his old grin. "It shouldn't be dull, anyway."

Then the businessman moved away, and Maggie found herself closer to Connor than she'd been in days. For a moment neither of them spoke, and then Connor glanced quickly over his shoulder as though they were being pursued. "If we're fast," he said, "we can get out to the kitchen without being noticed." He took her hand, and they managed to slip through the crowd successfully.

The kitchen was just as overrun as the rest of the house, with servants and hired caterers keeping the food and drink flowing, but Maggie and Connor finally found a relatively peaceful corner in the pantry. She smiled to see him lean against the counter and take in a deep breath like a drowning man coming up for air.

She knew it wasn't the time or the place for the closeness she longed for, but she couldn't keep herself from taking hold of his hand again. "You must be wrung out," she said sympathetically.

"Pretty nearly," he admitted. "I didn't think it was possible for me to wear a suit this many hours in a row."

"Well, if you want to loosen your tie, I'll keep it a secret," she said, and was heartened to see his grin return, this time with some spice to it.

"I'd better not," he said. "The temptation might be too much for me, and I still have another couple of hours of being respectable to do."

"And then you get to put your feet up for a little while, I hope," Maggie said. "This week must have been hard on all of you."

"It has," he said, "but unfortunately there's going to be precious little time to sit around with my feet up."

"Why is that?"

He rubbed a hand across his eyes, and the remnant of his grin faded. "It's a long story," he said, "and some of it concerns you. But I don't want to go into all the details now. Will you be home tomorrow, if I come by then?"

"I'll be free after three o'clock, when my baby-sitters get there," she told him. "This sounds serious, Connor. Does it have to do with Triple I?" She remembered the brief conversation she'd overheard at the punch table.

"Yes." Up to now, she knew the mention of the family company had annoyed him. But now he was looking positively animated about it. What had happened to change things?

Clearly, she'd have to wait for the answers—and for any further contact with Connor, it seemed. The maid, Cindy, was bearing down on them, apologizing for shooing them out of their hiding place but explaining that she needed the extra glasses on the top shelf.

"I'll get them," Connor offered, stretching his long arms up. "Where did all these people come from, anyway?"

"Your father had a lot of business contacts," Cindy explained, taking the box Connor handed her. "Thank you, Mr. Connor."

Connor raised his eyebrows as he watched Cindy walking away with the box. "I guess I have to learn about entertaining, as well as investing," he commented.

He looked as though he was contemplating kissing her, Maggie thought, but the kitchen staff whipping to and fro past the pantry was too great a distraction. "Come and see me tomorrow after three," Maggie murmured, squeezing his hand again as they left the kitchen for the even more crowded dining room. "Things will be calmer then."

"There'll be less of a crowd," he whispered back, "but I'm not sure 'calm' is what we're after." There was no missing what he meant, and the hunger in his eyes almost made up for the long week of being apart.

The doorbell rang the next day at precisely one minute after three, and Maggie smiled as she went to answer it.

"My baby-sitters just got here this minute," she told him.

"I know. I was sitting in the driveway waiting for them to show up." He stepped over the doorsill, and Maggie saw that he'd shed the hated suit and was wearing jeans again. His lightweight spring sports jacket looked new, though, and so did the off-white shirt underneath it.

"If I'd known you were out there, I would have invited you in. The kids have been asking me for days when we're going to play pick-up sticks for cash again."

He smiled, and put his arms around her. "Actually, I was glad of the time just to sit and wait," he said, as he buried his face in her hair. "Things have been too crazy lately. And there hasn't been nearly enough of this."

"This" was a kiss that took Maggie's breath away. She felt herself melt against Connor's body, aware of every point of contact between them. The smell of him was so familiar to her now, and it acted on her like a subtle perfume. She wanted more, wanted him to fill all of her senses with his loving.

"That's what I've been dreaming of all week," he said with a rough satisfaction. "Now, the only question is: do we sit and talk business first, or do I pick you up and carry you upstairs to the bedroom?"

Maggie moved a fraction of an inch closer to him, intimately aware of his need for her as his strong body pressed against hers. "Considering that my day-care kids are still here, and that Jordan's due home in an hour, maybe we should talk business first," she told him, smiling. "But don't think I'm not tempted."

"Good." He followed her into the living room.

Maggie pulled the curtains open a little further to catch the welcome spring sunshine, and her eye was caught by a shiny new Mercedes-Benz in her driveway. "Is that yours?" she asked in surprise. "What happened to the van?"

Connor leaned one arm against the mantel, in a gesture all too reminiscent of his stance the night they'd confronted one another in this room, and he'd finally come across with his secret. Maggie had a sudden uncomfortable sense of déjà vu, as though they might be stepping onto rocky ground again.

"I'm giving up the locksmith business," he announced casually. "I have a potential buyer, and he offered to buy the van and tools as part of the sale. So I decided I'd better get some new transportation."

Maggie took another look at the gleaming white car. "From black sheep to white knight," she speculated, only half in jest. "That's quite a switch, Connor." *And not the only one*, she added to herself, and waited for him to tell her more.

"Not as big a switch as you might think," he replied. "After what happened in Roxbury last weekend, I'd pretty much decided I'd had enough of midnight locksmith calls, anyway. I told you it had been losing its charm lately."

"And what will you do instead?" Maggie moved to the sofa and sat down, watching Connor closely.

"I'm going to run Triple I." He said the words as a challenge, daring her to be surprised.

"Full-time?"

He shrugged. "I guess it could turn into that. I'm not going to put that damned suit back on and spend all my time at the office, if that's what you're thinking."

"Well, at least I know it's still Connor Blake I'm talking to, then. But, Connor, why? You always said you hated Triple I."

He gave another little shrug. "What I hated about it was my father's insistence that I work there," he said. "Since he and I managed to work out a compromise on that point, and since, well, since he died, I guess I've been seeing things differently."

Maggie didn't say what immediately sprang to her mind—that perhaps Connor was trying to overcome the loss of his father by finally doing what his father had wanted. It was an extreme swing, but then, Connor Blake was an extreme kind of man.

"So I assume you're going to accept the chairmanship of the board," she ventured.

He smiled at her, and she wasn't sure she was quite comfortable with the look on his face. It had something of the cat and the canary to it.

"You bet I am," he said, "and I'm going to make some major changes in the place, believe me."

His cockiness made her nervous. "Connor," she said uncertainly, "you must have seen enough of Triple I when you worked there to know that it's not the kind of company that changes very fast, or very much."

"Well, it's going to have to now."

"In what way?"

"Its whole outlook, the whole way it does business. Triple I is a dinosaur, Maggie, a holdover from the days when wealthy people gave money to their banker friends and trusted them not to do foolish things with it. The investment market has changed since then, but Triple I hasn't."

"I think our clients may prefer the old-fashioned approach, to be honest with you."

He raised a black eyebrow at that. "'Our' clients?" he asked pointedly. "I never heard you sound so involved with the company before."

She fought to stay calm, battling the stubborn conviction that they were heading for a fight. "I am on the board of directors, after all," she said, "and that means I have to feel responsible for the company's policies. I'm not saying I agree or disagree with you, Connor, just that what you're proposing sounds as though it won't go over very well at Triple I."

There was an uncomfortable pause, and then he asked bluntly, "*Do* you agree with me, just out of interest? Or are you planning to vote on the traditional side at the meeting tonight?''

She'd forgotten that tonight was the second Monday of the month, or had assumed that with the recent upset of Kincaid's death, the second- and fourth-Monday-night board meetings would be rescheduled. Now she had to come up with an answer, and faster than she would have liked.

"I'm not sure," she said. "I'll have to hear exactly what you're proposing first."

"And hear what everybody else has to say against it, you mean," he said sharply.

They'd managed to get along so well together lately, Maggie thought unhappily, but now she could feel her temper starting to heat up again, the way it had at the beginning of their relationship. Why couldn't Connor Blake keep things on an even keel for five minutes at a time?

"I'm very much the junior member of the board," she pointed out to him, "and I don't know much about the business world. I only have a seat on the board because I inherited it from Grant. You know how the charter for Triple I works. Anyway, I guess I do tend to be swayed by the opinions of the other people on the board, but I'm not sure that's a bad thing. You don't need to make it sound as though I have no mind of my own."

He looked as though he was clenching his teeth on a harsh reply. "At least you agree to listen to my proposals?" he asked her.

"Of course I'll listen to them. I hope they'll work, Connor. I really do. But I can't vote with you just . . . because I love you."

She raised her eyes to his, realizing she'd never said the words to him before now. And now was the wrong time, she knew. Love didn't help them now, it only complicated things.

He was silent for a minute, and then he moved away from the fireplace and sat beside her on the sofa. She'd never met a man who could make her feel so many things at the same time, she thought—love and anger, misgivings and desire. Above all, desire . . .

She felt herself drawn to the warmth of him, and when he leaned closer to her, nothing else mattered just for the moment.

"Promise me one thing," he murmured.

"What's that?" She loved the way his deep voice could turn into that throaty whisper. It was the next thing to a caress.

"That you'll keep an open mind at the meeting tonight. I know there'll be plenty of opposition to anything new, but if I have even one person to back me up, things will be easier."

"I'll try, Connor. My mind will be as open as I can make it."

"Good." Then their closeness seemed to distract him as much as it did her, and he leaned even nearer and covered her mouth with a kiss that swept her into a warm, dark world of desire. She felt almost drugged with the sweetness of it, as she responded to the intimate searchings of his tongue and felt every nerve center in her body come alive at his touch. The real world could wait, she thought dazedly. This haze of pleasurable sensation was far too seductive to give up just at the moment.

The sound of the front door slamming brought their embrace to a quick end a few minutes later. "Hi, Mom," Jordan shouted, and Maggie raised her head long enough to call back, "Hi, honey. There's juice in the fridge if you want some."

She smoothed back Connor's dark hair from his forehead, aware that her own hair was probably in the same tangled state. "I wonder what Jordan thinks about the two of us," she said thoughtfully.

"Have you said anything to him about it?"

"No. I guess I wasn't sure what to tell him," she replied.

"How about, that we're in love with each other?" He leaned back against the leather sofa, watching her as she stood up and ran her fingers through her hair.

"Jordan's pretty perceptive. He's probably figured that out already," she said, with a brief smile. "In fact, it sounds like a lot of people have been putting two and two together on that score. But it's not quite that simple, Connor. What comes afterward?"

Neither of them seemed willing to answer that question, and Jordan's arrival in the living room a moment later was a more welcome interruption than Maggie would have admitted. They stuck to easier subjects over dinner, and it wasn't until six-thirty that the question of Triple I came back into the conversation.

"I should go up and get changed for the board meeting," she said, getting up from the kitchen table where they'd been eating chili and corn bread. "Are you planning to go home before the meeting, Connor?"

"What for?"

"Well, I thought . . . you're wearing jeans, and . . ." Awkwardly she let that sentence dangle, and rephrased what she was trying to say. "Board meetings are sort of formal occasions," she explained. "Your father always wore his best suit when he chaired them."

"Sounds just like Sunday dinners," Connor said laconically.

"I guess they're part of the same tradition." She noticed the glint in his eye, and heard that challenge in his tone again.

"Well, maybe it's time to start a few new traditions," was all he said.

"You're going to chair the meeting in jeans?"

"You sound shocked."

Maggie didn't like what he was implying. "Well, not really, but you'll raise some eyebrows, that's all."

"That's exactly what I intend to do. I didn't think yours would be among them."

Maggie frowned, willing her eyebrows to stay put. She knew she wasn't nearly as conservative as the other Triple I board members, but after five years of biweekly meetings with them, she *did* understand their point of view. Connor seemed to be planning to rock the boat in a serious way, and it made Maggie very uneasy. She realized with a sudden pang that what he was proposing could change the settled order of her life, and she wasn't sure she wanted that.

"Well, I'm still going to get changed," she told him. Once upstairs, in front of her closet, she had a hard time deciding what to wear. Anything too flamboyant or too casual would make Connor think she was backing him up in whatever crazy scheme he had up his sleeve. But anything too formal would put her squarely on the other side.

"Damn you, Connor Blake," she said out loud, finally pulling a simple ivory silk blouse and tan skirt from the closet. "Why do you have to go around turning everyone's lives upside down?"

Since all but one of the eight board members lived in or near Wellesley, they had decided many years ago not to make the trek all the way back into downtown Boston for their meetings. Instead, Edward Dennis, the bank manager, gave them the use of his branch's meeting room every second and fourth Monday evening. It was a pleasant, old-fashioned room, well-suited to the gathering of people who made up the Triple I board of directors. Connor's father, and Grant's, the company's founders, had written into the charter that membership on the board must stay in the family, and so all eight current members were related by blood or marriage to the original directors. Maggie had thought it a quaint custom at first, but over the years she'd come to see the sense of it. The board members cared personally about the fate of the company, and that had always worked to Triple I's benefit.

And now Connor intended to shake all that up. Maggie's stomach tightened a bit as they pulled into the bank parking lot in Connor's new Mercedes.

"I assume you have exactly the same position on the board as your father had," she said thoughtfully. "I mean, that as chairman you run the meetings, and if the board is split down the middle on something, your vote sways the count to one side or the other."

"That's right. Why do you ask?"

"Just refreshing my memory," Maggie hedged. In fact, she'd been going over the possibilities in her mind, trying to guess what might happen tonight. Since all she could safely predict was a fight of major proportions, she decided to give up fortune-telling for now.

Connor looked so confident as he strode beside her into the bank. She had to admit that the jeans-and-jacket combination suited him as the three-piece suit had never done. Still, she felt an unaccustomed flutter of nervousness as she walked beside him. A faint echo of her own past was troubling her and making her wary of Connor's new plan.

There were no empty chairs around the big table by the time she and Connor had taken their seats. Well, he'd been right about one thing already, she thought. Once the six other board members caught a glimpse of his casual attire, all twelve eyebrows were raised in short order.

Maggie did a quick inventory of the six faces. Maria Blake was at the end of the table where she'd always sat, next to the chairman's seat. Her face showed the strain that the past week had been for her. Next to her, Caroline Lewis looked as serene as ever, except for her faint look of surprise when she saw Connor. Talbot Hughes, an old friend of both families, looked contemptuous in a way that would have done Kincaid Blake himself proud.

Connor's brother-in-law, Richard, sat on Maggie's side of the table, next to the other younger member of the board, Gerry Williams. Gerry's father had been Triple I's first treasurer, and Gerry had inherited his seat on the board, as

Maggie had. The bank manager, Mr. Dennis, filled the eighth and last seat at the table.

"It's good to see everyone here," Connor began, sounding as relaxed as though he'd been doing this all his life. "This is an important meeting for us, and I'd like to start my job as chairman of the board by pointing this company in some new directions."

Maggie saw the growing surprise on the six faces. It only added to her sense of unease.

"I want to make my position clear from the very beginning," Connor said. "If I'm going to be at the head of this organization, its policies are going to have to change, and change radically."

Maggie heard rumblings from Talbot Hughes's corner. The words "change" and "radical" affected Talbot the way a red flag affected a bull.

"Triple I has always been known as a safe, solid, secure company. And it's made a decent profit over the years. But times are changing, and there are lots of new investment opportunities out there that we should be taking advantage of. It's time to look farther afield, and that's just the direction I intend to take us in."

"What kind of opportunities are you talking about?" Gerry Williams's quiet voice sounded as unsure as Maggie felt.

Connor had clearly done his homework in the last couple of weeks. He spoke at length about new possibilities for investing their clients' money—everything from new computer software companies to films. As he worked his way through his list, Maggie saw the growing dismay in the board members' faces.

"All of those things sound risky to me," Maria Blake ventured, when he was done.

"They're risky fields, yes, but also very lucrative ones, if you're smart about where you invest."

"And who at Triple I has that kind of expertise?" Edward Dennis demanded.

"Not very many people, yet. That's a big part of this plan. If we're going to expand our horizons, we need to lure new people into the company."

"*If* we're going to expand," Talbot Hughes echoed darkly.

"I'm committed to changing the personality of this company," Connor replied smoothly, "and I'm prepared to fight for it, if I have to."

That was laying all the cards on the table with a vengeance, Maggie thought. Now they'd see some fireworks.

She was right. "I can't back you up on that, Connor," Edward Dennis said. "Triple I's whole appeal to investors has been that it's a safe, dependable place to put your money. I can't see our current clients trusting us to branch off in wild directions."

"We'll be attracting new clients with a new policy," Connor returned.

"And losing old ones," Talbot Hughes grunted.

"I don't think so. Not once we've established that we know what we're doing."

"How long will that take?" Caroline Lewis asked reasonably. "We can't just change our image overnight."

"I realize that," Connor said. "And I'm not talking about doing anything overnight. We'll prove to people gradually that broadening our reach is a good idea, and I'm willing to bet we don't lose a single client in the process."

"You seem willing to bet on a number of things, young man," Talbot Hughes interjected. "Would you be so willing to bet your own money, or just other people's?"

Connor's dark face flushed slightly, and Maggie could see him trying to keep his temper under control. "Since I have large blocks of Triple I stock myself, I'm taking a risk along with you and all our clients, Talbot," he said.

"There are plenty of investment firms out there specializing in short-term, high-risk investments," Connor's brother-in-law stated. "I say we should leave those fields to them and stick with what we're good at."

"Why shouldn't we be good at both?" Connor demanded. "We have the resources to do it."

Every word Connor spoke was touching on Maggie's most uncomfortable memories. She'd been a small child when her father had left the family behind, but she remembered so many arguments between her parents that sounded just like this one. "Why can't you just put the money in the bank for once?" her mother would demand, over and over, and her father would always reply that this scheme was a winner that was certain to make them all rich.

She crossed her arms tightly. She'd known from the beginning that Connor Blake was a reckless dreamer, and she'd loved him for it. But maybe he was taking things too far now. The thought made her insides twist uncomfortably.

"If you're hot to expand, why not consider opening new offices?" Gerry Williams was asking. "That could be a way to increase profits without changing the character of the company."

Connor leaned forward, palms flat on the table. He was standing, dominating his audience. "The whole point is that I intend to change the character of the company," he told them. "I don't want to preside over a firm that hasn't done anything new in sixty years. This is a different game now, Gerry."

"Game!" Talbot Hughes snorted.

Maggie stayed silent through the whole exchange. She knew they were approaching the inevitable moment when they would have to put this to a vote.

The moment arrived, and with it the end of Connor's patience. Maggie could see the effort it was costing him to stay calm as he announced, "We're going to put this to a vote. And please bear in mind that as chairman, I can bring this issue up again and again, if I choose."

They were all bearing it in mind, Maggie could tell. There was no doubt, from the determination on his face, that

Connor wasn't going to let this question drop on the basis of a single meeting.

"We'll go around the table," Connor said, taking his seat for the first time that evening. "Talbot, you're first."

"And I'm dead against this whole scheme," the old man said positively. "Kincaid must be turning over at the very idea, and you know it."

"A simple yea or nay will do," Connor said dryly, and Edward Dennis, the board's secretary, recorded Talbot's vote.

Caroline Lewis was next. "I'm sorry to say this, Connor, but I have to vote against the idea, too," she said. "Maybe I'm just being cautious, but our clients trust us with their money, and I wouldn't like to do anything that might abuse that trust, even slightly."

Edward Dennis recorded another "nay." Maria Blake echoed Caroline's words, adding, "I can't help thinking that your father—" She couldn't finish the sentence but held her handkerchief to her trembling lips, and Caroline Lewis put a reassuring hand on her old friend's shoulder. Maggie saw the spasm of regret cross Connor's handsome face, but when it came his turn to vote, he was adamant in backing his own proposal.

Gerry Williams, Edward Dennis and Richard Westborough all registered their negative votes. Maggie, at the end of the long table, was Connor's last hope for support, and everyone knew it. With even one board member backing him, his position would be strengthened. And far more important than the investment company was the question of Maggie's personal support, she knew.

She took a deep breath. Connor's smoldering gaze was as seductive as it ever was, reminding her fiercely of what the two of them had started to build together, and pleading with her not to let him down. She wanted desperately to trust him. She *did* trust him, with so many things.

But that uneasy voice inside her wouldn't leave her alone. She pictured Connor forcing his new ideas on Triple I and having things go sour. If the firm faltered, so much would be lost: not just their clients' money, but Connor's fortune and Jordan's inheritance. And the whole settled life Maggie had grown so used to.

When she thought of Jordan having to grow up tough and jaded as she had, the nervousness inside her clenched into something that felt like a fist. She just couldn't afford to take the kind of risk Connor was proposing.

"I have to vote no." She forced the words out and felt her heart start to beat a little faster now that she'd actually done it. Connor's face didn't change, but his eyes darkened in anger, and Maggie couldn't keep her own eyes locked with his.

"Well, I guess that's that." Talbot Hughes sounded smug, and Maggie wished she could kick him.

"No, that is *not* necessarily that." Connor stood slowly, his manner showing clearly that the meeting was over. "We meet again in two weeks, and I intend to bring the matter up again, with more information to back me up, if that's what it takes. And in the meantime—" that black-eyed gaze grabbed Maggie's eyes, and held them "—in the meantime, I guess I have some negotiating to do."

Nine

He started negotiating on the way down the stairs. Maggie was considering asking Mrs. Blake if she could get a lift home in the Blake family car, which she knew would be in the parking lot with a uniformed driver in attendance to take the two older women home. But before she got a chance to ask, Connor was at her heels with an insistent hand under her elbow.

"Let's get into the car, and make it snappy," he was saying. "I don't feel like hanging around and chatting."

"I can believe that," she said, and let him guide her down the stairs to the parking lot.

The air outside was balmy, but Maggie still felt chilled. The expression in Connor's eyes and her own tension haunted her. He didn't give vent to his feelings until they were in the car and driving back toward her house, but the silence between them was icy, and it was almost a relief when he finally spoke.

Almost.

"What the hell do you think you're up to?" he demanded suddenly, turning the wheel hard as he made a left turn. "I thought I heard you say you were going to keep an open mind."

"Maybe I just didn't trust your ideas enough to vote for them."

He slammed an angry hand against the wheel. "This from a woman who admits she knows very little about the investment business," he muttered.

Maggie was silent, not sure she wanted to tell him that her decision had been based more on her gut feelings than any business sense she possessed. But she might have known that Connor would be one jump ahead of her, even here.

"Why do I get the feeling there's more going on here than just concern for Triple I?" he asked, as he pulled into Maggie's driveway. When she didn't answer right away, he turned the engine off and rephrased his question. "What were your real reasons for voting against me, Maggie?"

She wasn't sure she could explain it to him, or that it would make any sense if she did. She sidestepped the question, wishing he would stop looking at her with those penetrating dark eyes.

"I don't see why my vote is so important to you," she told him. "Even if I'd voted for you, it wouldn't have changed anyone else's mind. And you need three votes to carry the board, not just one."

He half turned in his seat, and she could feel herself being drawn toward him. She resisted that seductive pull, but she knew it was still there as he spoke. "Did you consider that your vote is important to me for reasons that have nothing to do with Triple I?" he asked in a low voice.

"You mean you wanted me to vote for you because... because of us?"

He reached out and took her hand. She knew her fingers felt cold, but no matter how much she wanted him to warm her with his love, she still couldn't ignore that nagging voice of experience that had kept her from supporting Connor this evening.

"Yes, because of us," he echoed. "And that's why it's so important that I know why you objected so strongly to what I was trying to say tonight."

He didn't push her, but gave her time to think. Maggie forced in a deep breath, trying to steady her uneasy nerves. "I think you're right," she admitted. "But I'm still not sure it will fix anything." She took another breath, and then said matter-of-factly, "I've told you that my father was the kind of person who could never resist a good scheme for making money. And he always seemed to lose more than he made."

"Are you telling me that because your father—"

She held up a hand to stop him. "Just listen to me. I'm not talking about some detached, academic experience here. My mother and I went through some very tough times when I was young as a direct result of my father's crazy plans." Her voice was trembling now, but she made herself go on. "And I refuse to take that same chance with my own life and Jordan's."

She saw the muscles in his jaw move as he clenched his teeth. Abruptly he let go of her hand, grasping the steering wheel again instead. When he spoke, he sounded as though he was having the same struggle she was in speaking calmly. "I think you're letting some unhappy memories dictate what you think," he said finally. "That's emotion talking, Maggie, not common sense."

"It's common sense, all right," she flashed back. She'd hoped he would understand, but even if he didn't, she had to let her own feelings guide her. "It's sense that I learned the hard way. And I won't go through that again or put my son through it."

"In other words, anything that jeopardizes your nice safe lifestyle—" he waved a hand dismissively at the big brick house in front of them "—is something you don't want to hear about."

"If I think it's too risky, yes." She was beginning to feel angry now, and she welcomed the feeling.

"Do you really think I'd start throwing people's money around just for the hell of it?"

"I think maybe you're rushing into a field you aren't all that familiar with. You've admitted that yourself," she reminded him.

"I've also done a lot of research in the recent past," he pointed out. "And I do like to succeed at things, Maggie."

His eyes were burning into hers now, trying to change her mind. Maggie thought about his single-minded strength of character. He was right; once he'd set his mind to something, he would try to move heaven and earth to get what he wanted. Was that bullishness enough to forge a new identity for Triple I? For a moment it was tempting to give in to the hunger in his eyes and tell him he had her vote of support.

Then she felt all over again the bleakness of growing up with no money and no hope, and she knew that simple desire for Connor Blake wasn't enough to convince her. She shook her head slowly, torn between a present love and a painful past.

"I'm sorry, Connor," she whispered. "I just can't see it your way."

She watched the anger building in his face like a storm cloud, and wished she could soften her rejection somehow. "I love you and I love the way you do things," she said, "but I just think you're trying to operate in the wrong world now."

"Do you really?" His eyes darkened suddenly, telling her she'd hurt him without meaning to. "In that case, we don't have anything more to negotiate about, do we? I thought we'd gotten past all this, but I can see I was wrong."

There seemed to be nothing more to say. Maggie stepped out of the car, racking her brain for some compromise to get them talking again, but for the life of her she couldn't think of one. The subject, like Connor's dark face, was closed.

"Goodbye, then, Connor," she said uncertainly.

"Goodbye." The two syllables had an ugly sound of finality that made her shiver inside. He couldn't really mean it. They meant too much to each other to throw everything away like this. But then, as she'd already pointed out to herself, Connor Blake was an extreme kind of man.

And it was an extreme kind of pain that she carried inside herself as she walked up the long driveway and into her house, alone.

"Heard anything from K.C. lately, Maggie?"

Bobbie Lewis helped herself to another slice of roast beef and looked pointedly across the Lewis family table at her sister-in-law.

"His name's Connor now," Jordan chimed in.

"You're right. When you get as old as I am, you can't always remember all these little details." Bobbie, who was a ripe, old thirty-six, winked at her nephew. "Anyway, I was wondering if you'd seen anything of him lately."

"Not since last Monday's board meeting," Maggie said, trying to speak lightly. The mention of Connor's name made the hurt she'd been feeling leap up inside her all over again. She'd been trying to stay calm, not wanting to bring the whirlwind of her own feelings into the sedate atmosphere of the family Sunday dinner, but she knew from a glance in the front-hall mirror on her way in that her turmoil was showing in her face. The slight circles under her eyes proclaimed her restless nights, and her eyes looked troubled.

"I saw him the other day," Caroline Lewis said unexpectedly. "He dropped in for tea one afternoon. He wanted to talk about Triple I."

"I wish he'd drop in at our house," Jordan said. "He'd have to talk about something more interesting, though." Jordan was as bored by Triple I as Connor had been until recently, Maggie thought.

"Oh, this was interesting enough." Caroline smiled serenely. "He was trying to enlist my sympathy for the changes he wants to make at Triple I. He put it very persuasively, too, I must admit."

"What did you tell him?" Maggie couldn't help asking.

"Oh, of course I couldn't support him, not when he wants to turn the whole place on its head like that. But he was very civil about it."

More than he was with me, Maggie thought unhappily. But then she knew where Connor's anger had sprung from. Her approval meant more to him than any of the other board members' did. The pain she'd been dealing with all week seemed to stab through her again.

"I just mentioned him because I had a visit from him, too, down at the store," Bobbie said, touching her linen napkin to her mouth. "You'll never guess what he wanted."

"Some new clothes," Jordan said, taking his aunt literally.

Bobbie smiled at him. "Close, little pal," she said. "He wanted to talk about clothes. Specifically, investing in fashion. He had some guy with him who was supposed to be an expert in the field."

"Did he sound like he knew what he was talking about?" Maggie asked. "The expert, I mean."

"You're asking the wrong person. You know the language of investment capital might as well be Greek to me. K.C.—I mean Connor—seemed very into it, though."

"He seems to be doing a great deal of work on this idea of his," Caroline said thoughtfully. "It's a pity because I don't think he's ever going to change the minds of anyone on the board."

"When I saw Connor after Uncle Blake's funeral, he told me about this great kind of dog," Jordan said, apparently feeling the talk of Triple I had gone on long enough.

"What kind of dog?" Maggie asked.

"I can't remember the name. Air-something."

"Airedale?" Bobbie suggested.

"Yeah. And he said Mom would probably go for it because it doesn't shed hair all over the place."

He was watching his mother astutely, and Maggie had to work hard to keep her eyes from swimming with sudden tears. Only a week ago things had seemed almost settled between her and Connor, to the extent, apparently, that he'd been ready to join in with Jordan's lobbying for a dog. And now— "Airedales are pretty big, honey," she said, hoping her voice sounded steady.

"Well, our house is pretty big," Jordan pointed out reasonably. "Connor said he would talk to you about it. Did he, Mom?"

"No," she said. "Not yet, anyway. Are you done with your roast beef, honey, or are you going to finish that last bite?"

Jordan turned his attention to the last bite of beef, clearly aware that the subject was being changed. Maggie wondered whether her emotions were plain to everyone at the table. Maybe Caroline and Bobbie were just politely looking the other way, which was, of course, the well-bred thing to do. Half of Maggie was grateful for that because it kept them from asking her awkward questions. But half of her wanted madly to escape from this well-mannered Sunday setting, back to the world of unfettered feelings and sensations she'd shared with Connor.

Instead, she ate a small helping of sherry trifle, the traditional Sunday dessert, and wished she knew what she should do next.

She left Jordan at the Lewis house, where he'd been invited to stay overnight in Bobbie's coachhouse apartment. It was a treat for both Jordan and Bobbie, but when Maggie arrived home by herself, she missed Jordan's chatter more than she usually did. The brick house felt very empty to her as she busied herself with a few housekeeping jobs she hadn't gotten to earlier in the week. Maybe she *should* get a dog after all, she thought.

Then she shook her head, stopping to think with the kitchen floor half-mopped. What she should do first was patch things up with Connor. She still couldn't see any clear way to resolve their differences, but she knew she didn't want to spend any more time apart. Her longing for him was more powerful than anything else.

She stood the mop up in the bucket, and tiptoed across the still-damp floor to the phone. She dialed Connor's number, but there was no answer. After five rings she hung up and went back to her mopping with a frown on her face.

At 11:00 she tried again. There was still no answer. Where could he be? She knew, from a brief conversation with Maria Blake, that he wasn't staying at the family home in Wellesley. And he'd given up his all-night locksmith job. But when she called again at 11:30 just before she went to bed, once again she heard the phone ringing unanswered.

The house felt emptier than ever to Maggie when she awoke at two. She was aware of the faint sounds the heating system made as it came on, and of the new leaves rustling in the trees in the backyard. She closed her eyes again, and Connor's image confronted her so strongly that for a moment she could almost hear his steady breathing beside her in the big bed, the way she'd heard it two weekends ago in Connor's loft apartment.

She rolled over in bed, reaching for the telephone before common sense could talk her out of it. She and Connor belonged together, no matter what their differences, and she had to find him and tell him so before too many things could come between them.

She held her breath while the phone rang once, twice, and then on the third ring he answered.

"Hello?"

"Connor, this is Maggie."

There was a long silence. Maggie wondered if the beating of her heart was clearly audible over the telephone wires. Then he said, "What are you doing up at this hour?" She couldn't tell whether he was still angry with her or not.

"I'm not really up. I mean I'm awake, but I'm still horizontal."

"Horizontal, meaning in bed?"

"Yes." Her pulse accelerated as though he had turned on a switch.

"Hmm." The warmly speculative sound was the most welcome thing she'd heard from him in a week.

"I tried to call you earlier tonight, but there was no answer," she told him. "But then I remembered that for the past ten years you've been living your life upside down, and you probably weren't going to get out of the habit of being awake at night all of a sudden."

He actually chuckled. "Good guess," he admitted. "As a matter of fact, I've spent the last few nights at my workbench because you're absolutely right—it feels strange to me to be in bed when it's dark. I just unplugged my phone earlier. I was tired of getting irate calls from Talbot Hughes."

She took a sudden deep breath and let her common sense fly out the window. They could sort out their differences in the daylight, but for now, the only thing that seemed to matter was that they be together.

"Would you like some company, since you're not sleeping?" she asked him. The thought of it made her quiver in some very well-remembered places.

"Maggie..."

His voice held all the hunger she knew so well from their early encounters, and it acted on her just as powerfully. Whatever stood in their way, it didn't matter for the moment.

"Jordan's away for the night," she said breathlessly, already putting her feet over the edge of her bed. "I can be there in twenty minutes."

"All the way from Wellesley?" His voice teased her, caressed her.

She smiled. "I can find my way out of Wellesley in a hurry, when I have to," she told him.

He was waiting for her in the parking lot. At first Maggie thought he was just being considerate, thinking of the riskiness of the neighborhood at night. But when she stepped out of the car and into his arms, she realized it was because he was just as eager as she was, maybe more.

"You look tired," he said, as he held her close.

"So do you." She looked up into his face. There was a new weariness in the stubborn lines of his brows.

"Just trying to adjust to this crazy schedule, I guess," he said lightly.

"You mean the crazy schedule of being awake in the daytime and asleep at night?"

"That's the one. I don't know how you daytime types manage."

He kept a strong arm around her as they walked up to his apartment. Inside, the big open space was only dimly lit. A small tabletop lamp made a pool of light next to the sofa, and a shop light illuminated the workbench. The bench top was strewn with drawings and the same mysterious electronic items Maggie had noticed before.

"You've been busy," she commented.

He shrugged. Maggie could feel his muscles through the blue chambray shirt he wore over his jeans, and it heightened her own eagerness for him. "It passes the time," he said offhandedly.

"Well, I have other ideas for passing the time," she whispered, standing on her toes as she wrapped her arms around his neck. He let out a long breath that was almost a groan, and clasped her hungrily to him.

"I wondered if I'd ever hold you like this again," he muttered against her ear.

"It feels too good to give up," she replied. His lips were brushing her cheek now, and her words ended on a little gasp of pleasure.

"Far too good."

She'd dressed herself in thirty seconds flat, omitting such unnecessary items as underwear. Now, when Connor circled the waistband of her jeans with his broad palms and then slid his hands slowly upward inside her loose blue sweatshirt, his searching fingers encountered the smoothness of her unfettered breasts. She moaned softly as he captured them in his grip and ran his thumbs knowingly over their taut centers.

"You don't know what that does to me," she murmured.

His lips curved into that devil's grin. "I know exactly what it does to you," he replied. He was still grinning as his lips met hers, and then the grin dissolved into a sweet and hungry passion when he felt her mouth open to him, inviting him with its warmth. Without taking his lips from hers, he lifted her off her feet and carried her into the bedroom.

There, too, a single lamp made a soft glow in the darkness. Maggie felt as though this moment together was theirs alone, while the rest of the world slept.

He laid her down on the bed and eased his long frame down beside her. Maggie pulled her sweatshirt over her head and felt everything inside her pulse a little more urgently when she saw the unmistakable look of longing in Connor's eyes. His hand made a long sweep across her body, and suddenly even the aching pleasure of being touched by him was not enough for Maggie. She needed to feel him wrapped around her in the most intimate embrace imaginable, filling her as only he had ever done.

She reached up to undo the buttons on his shirt, and pushed it from his broad shoulders. He seemed to share her sudden urgency, and shed the rest of his clothes quickly.

"I've wanted you so much," she whispered. She let her eyes, and then her hands, travel over his magnificent body, following the strong, curving planes of his muscled chest and the long lines of his thighs. His response to her touch was so immediate that Maggie became bolder, marveling all over again how they seemed to have been made to love each other.

"Oh, God, Maggie." His voice was ragged, filled with passion. His fingers reached for the waistband of her jeans, making short work of the button and zipper, and then sliding them with a deliberate slowness down her legs. When they had joined his in a crumpled pile on the floor, he began working his way back up again, this time turning his face against the smoothness of the skin at the crook of her knee, the warm expanse of her inner thigh, and higher...

The knowing, caressing warmth of his mouth touched off explosions inside Maggie, propelling her beyond mere pleasure. She'd never dreamed of a touch as intimate as this, or known what a world of sensation was captured inside her own body. He took her higher and higher, as expertly as a master musician might have created a whole world of sound, and then, when she'd lost all thoughts of anything but the burning need inside her, he moved to cover her completely, and filled her with one deep thrust that answered every longing she'd felt for him.

Her legs were locked around his, and her arms circled his broad shoulders, as though she was searching for a closeness that would never end. With every movement they were joined more fully, until their moving together became a force neither of them could resist, a pulsing rhythm carrying them on and on...

Just as Maggie had the fleeting notion that she wanted to keep moving like this forever, everything inside her suddenly contracted into a vast circle of light, and she heard Connor's hoarse cry mingling with her own, telling her that he, too, had reached the brink of whatever abyss they'd been propelling each other toward. For a long, shuddering moment they were almost motionless, and then Maggie began to breathe again.

Connor seemed as reluctant to move or speak as she was, and Maggie knew the reason why. This shared moment in the middle of the night was not endless, after all. They still had problems to overcome, and both of them knew it. They held each other close now, not speaking, postponing the inevitable time when real life would enter their lives again.

"I guess you have to work later on this morning, don't you?" Connor asked finally, moving to one side and looking down at her with dark eyes that were still clouded with passion.

"I guess so." Maggie glanced at the bedside clock. It was after three. "In five hours, to be exact. What about you?"

"I have to be somewhere at eight-thirty." He didn't seem to want to go into detail.

"You really have given up your locksmith business, haven't you?" she asked him.

"Yep. Sold the whole thing, lock, stock and barrel."

"Will you miss it?"

His face grew more serious as he considered the question. "I'll miss being my own boss," he said.

She didn't have an answer to that one. She knew too well what had prompted it, and after the sheer magic of their lovemaking just a few minutes ago, she hated to break the spell with talk of Triple I. Yet that was what they needed desperately to talk about.

Connor, too, seemed to shy away from the problem. He looked at the clock and said, "Are you feeling sleepy?"

"A little. And I know I will be by mid-morning, if I don't try to get some rest now."

"I was just thinking the same thing." He was reaching for the covers as he spoke, pulling the light wool blanket over both of them. "Maybe I should set the alarm. How does seven o'clock sound?"

"It sounds terrible, but I'm afraid you'll have to make it even earlier. I'm going to have to fight rush-hour traffic going home."

He set the clock for six and turned out the bedside lamp. Maggie gave herself up to a pleasant drowsiness still half-tinged with passion, snuggling herself against his warm, strong body. She knew this state of mind had nothing to do with reality, but reality, she decided sleepily, could just wait till 6:00 a.m.

Ten

It can't be six already," she groaned, a mere three hours later. "I feel like I've only been asleep for five minutes."

"Me, too." Connor yawned, stretching his arms, and then settled them back around Maggie. "I don't think I've ever been more tempted to play hooky."

"I'm not even going to let myself be tempted. Those kids are going to start arriving on my doorstep at eight, and I've got to be there."

Maggie pulled herself reluctantly from Connor's embrace and stepped out of bed. Her jeans and sweatshirt were still in a heap on the floor.

"Guess you have to get home and get some underwear on before then, too," Connor teased, lying back in the bed with his hands behind his head.

She grinned at him and caught her breath all over again at the rugged beauty of his shoulders and the strength of his arms. This gypsy of hers was the most appealing man she'd ever encountered, she thought. Was it really possible that he could ever fit into her world?

"Some underwear is definitely in order," she agreed, running her fingers through her hair and thinking that a shower wasn't a bad idea, either. Then she took a deep breath and looked directly at him. "What have you got planned for today, Connor?" she asked.

His dark eyes narrowed. "Just some appointments," he said.

"To do with Triple I, I suppose?"

"Yes, as a matter of fact." He was deliberately noncommittal, daring her to push the subject further.

She thought of the lonely nights of the past week and decided she had to dare it. "About the company, Connor..." she began.

"Yes?" His face was still blank, as though he was being careful not to get too deeply into the subject.

"Well, I've been thinking a lot about what I said to you last Monday night. About worrying that your plans would lose money for the company, I mean." He didn't answer, but she thought she saw a faint glimpse of hope in his eyes. "I—I think maybe you were right about me, that I've been letting my own experiences color my judgement. And for a while there, I lost track of the main point."

"And what is that?" His voice was low and vibrant.

"That you and I should be together." She looked him straight in the eye as she spoke, feeling the ever-present tug of attraction between them. "I love you, Connor. I don't want to be apart from you anymore."

He didn't move, but the look in his eyes told her how much her words meant to him. Quickly, she went on, "And I've been thinking a lot about Triple I, too. I'm willing to back your new plan now, if you think you can present it in a way that the board members can swallow."

"Diplomacy has never been my strong suit," he said with a self-deprecating grin.

"Tell me about it," Maggie smiled back.

"What are you suggesting?"

Maggie sat down on the edge of the bed and put her arms around his shoulders. He smelled musky and sweet all at the same time, and it brought faint echoes of their lovemaking to Maggie's mind. "I haven't thought out a lot of details yet," she told him. "And I really do have to run if I'm going to get home by eight. Why don't you come for dinner tonight and we can talk about it?"

"I'm tied up tonight with the guy who bought my locksmith business. How about Tuesday?"

"Fine. No, sorry, it's not. I have to take Jordan to a swim meet Tuesday."

"Wednesday, then."

"Wednesday. And bring that stack of plans you've got on your workbench. I'm betting there's something in them that we can sell to Triple I."

To her surprise, it wasn't hard to stay awake that day. But it *was* nearly impossible to keep her mind on her work. Luckily she'd already prepared lots of things for the kids to do from eight till three, because her mind kept straying to thoughts of making love with Connor and the hopes she had for their future together. What she'd told him was true; her love for him had grown to be stronger than her fears about his new plans for Triple I.

But that didn't mean those fears had vanished, and mixed in with everything else she was feeling, there was still an undercurrent of anxiety about the whole situation. And there was something about Connor himself this morning that had made her nervous. She'd had the feeling he was deliberately holding himself back, not yet committing everything to the new life he'd chosen. Given the cool reception he'd gotten at the Triple I meeting, Maggie could understand why he would stay a little aloof, hedging his bets. But she wondered if the family black sheep was really ready to join the family again—the family that included her.

Those thoughts were still worrying her on Wednesday, when Connor arrived for dinner with a book about dogs for Jordan and an armload of information that he'd gathered in his researches for Triple I. He'd apparently decided that the best approach was to overwhelm the board with facts until they conceded that he did, in fact, know what he was talking about.

"I'm not sure that's the best way to do it," Maggie said.

"Why not? If they want information, I'll give them a ton of it."

"That may be too much like your initial approach," Maggie told him. "It's so overwhelming, like asking them to sink or swim all at once."

"Then what do you suggest?" He asked the question grudgingly, but at least he asked it.

"What about settling on just one project to start with? Something new, but not too terribly different from the kinds of things Triple I has invested in up till now."

Connor looked at the mountain of paper that covered Maggie's living-room table. "Got any suggestions?"

"Not yet, but it shouldn't be too hard to pick one."

It turned out to be harder than she'd thought. There was nothing that she felt sure all the board members would feel confident about, although she and Connor spent the hour before dinner searching for one. After dinner, it was easy to ignore the stack of paper and get involved in a backyard baseball game with Jordan. And after Jordan had gone to bed, Maggie and Connor let themselves get caught up in a movie on the television, which kept Maggie up long past her normal bedtime.

"It's all very well for you," she yawned, as they were saying protracted goodbye at the door. "But I need more than four hours of sleep if I'm going to function." Her arms were wrapped around his neck, and she breathed in deeply as he kissed the soft skin of her neck. "One of these nights I should get around to repaying hospitality and invite you to stay here," she murmured.

"One of these nights," he said lightly, and both of them knew that it wouldn't be tonight. So much more was involved than just a night of pleasure together—it involved Jordan and Connor's new position in Maggie's family and his own—and none of that had been really settled yet. Maggie was managing to keep her own fears at bay, but she couldn't forget the way Connor was still keeping his distance, holding back in some subtle but important ways.

It was Saturday by the time they got back to work on Connor's slate of proposed new investments. Maggie and Jordan paid a visit to the big loft apartment, and while Jordan inspected Connor's workbench, Maggie and Connor tackled the pile of paper again. To Maggie's dismay there was still no clear choice among the dozens of ideas.

"If we pick the right one, we could sell them on the whole idea," she said, frowning. "But if it's not just right, it'll only confirm their suspicions that the idea won't work."

"Hey, Connor," Jordan said for the fourth time, "what's this thing?"

Connor patiently explained the item to Jordan. He was far more patient with kids than he was with adults, Maggie had already noticed. It was too bad he hadn't used that same tone of voice when speaking to the board on Monday night.

"That's the gizmo that makes this whole alarm system work," he was saying, connecting one of the pieces of electronic equipment on his workbench to a long series of wires. "See, this is the brains of the operation. It controls sensors at the ends of all these wires. And it's programmable for eight different settings."

"So you can go away for eight days and have your lights go on and off at different times every day," Jordan said.

"Right. But here's the beauty of it. You can also hook it up to your telephone and change the program even when you're away from home. See?"

He pushed a few buttons, and Maggie heard Jordan exclaiming over the magic of the numbers that seemed to change themselves. Then she sat up straighter, watching Connor closely.

"Connor," she said, "how much money would it take to manufacture those security systems in quantity?"

He looked over his shoulder, still absorbed in explaining things to Jordan. "Haven't any idea," he said offhandedly. "Why? You think Triple I should invest in it?"

"Yes," she said firmly. "That's exactly what I think."

The bluntness of his answer took her by surprise. "No," he said unequivocally. Even Jordan looked startled at the sudden force in Connor's tone.

"But why not? It would be perfect for—"

"No, Maggie. I've got a hundred other potential investments for Triple I lined up. There's no need to bring my own work into it."

He was so adamant that Maggie let the subject drop. But an hour later, when they'd finished looking through those hundred potential projects and still nothing ideal had cropped up, she returned to her idea.

"Look at it this way," she said. "If there's one thing the people at Triple I trust, it's the Blake name. If they know you'll be running this alarm company, they'll be more likely to back it."

"They sure didn't seem to trust the Blake name last Monday night," he muttered. "They acted like I was planning to ruin the firm right there on the spot."

"They were in shock," Maggie said. "And you have to admit you did present things very suddenly. But this—"

She was standing next to Connor at the workbench, looking at his careful drawings for the alarm system. "All you'd have to do is present this as you've drawn it up, and I'm sure they'd be very impressed."

He seemed to be considering it, but then without warning he started rolling the plans up, securing them with a rubber band as though he wanted them to stay well-kept secrets. "No," he said again. "It won't work, Maggie."

She had a sneaking feeling there was more behind his refusal than just pessimism about its chances of success with
the board. "But why?" she persisted. "Why won't you even
consider it?"

He turned his head slowly to look at her, and she didn't
like the shuttered look in his eyes. It was that same sense of
holding back she'd worried about earlier, but now it was
intensified and she thought she knew why.

She was right. "I don't want to mix my private life with
Triple I," he said, almost reluctant to admit it. "This is
something I've created for myself. It has nothing to do with
the family business."

He glanced around his apartment, down the length of his
well-equipped workbench. Maggie had a disconcerting sense
that he was feeling too much like his young self again,
trapped by the pressure of family tradition and desperately
trying to forge a life of his own. If that was the case . . .

"Sounds like you're having some second thoughts about
all of this," she said softly.

He didn't answer right away but went on putting away the
plans and components he'd taken out to show Jordan.
When he finally spoke, he didn't meet her eyes. "I'm not
having second thoughts," he said, and she could sense the
strength of his willpower behind the phrase. "I just don't
want to have Triple I getting involved in this particular project, that's all."

And that, clearly, was all for the moment. Maggie decided to let it drop, but her heart was heavy as she and Jordan drove back to Wellesley. The closer she and Connor got
to love, it seemed, the more the difficulties of the past rose
up to meet them.

She didn't hear from him again until late Monday afternoon, two hours before the Triple I board meeting. "I'm
sorry I haven't called," he began.

"That's all right," she said, keeping her voice neutral in
spite of the almost nonstop thinking she'd been doing about

the problem of Connor Blake. "I happened to be awake at three a.m. yesterday, and I almost called you then."

"I wish you had." His voice sounded strained and less certain than usual. "I miss you, Maggie."

"I miss you, too." Maggie gripped the receiver tightly, holding on to the hope that they might finally find a way out of this impasse. "I guess I'll see you tonight at the meeting."

"Actually, that was what I called about. I've been thinking about your suggestion, about presenting my alarm system as an investment opportunity to the board."

Maggie held her breath, waiting for him to go on.

"I've been taking a hard look at why I was so adamant about not considering the idea," he said. "And I think it has to do with the whole way I feel about getting back into the family again."

"I thought it might be tied up with that," Maggie said gently. Could this mean he was ready to enter more fully into the life that was waiting for him? She tightened her grip on the receiver.

"Well, I think it is. But Maggie, you've got to understand just how stifled the whole family scene has always made me feel."

Maggie's heart sank. He sounded apologetic but still firm in what he was saying. "It doesn't need to stifle you any more," she said, trying to stay calm. "You're the one in control now, and you don't have to let those old traditions tie you down if you don't want them to."

There was a long pause, and then he said, "I'm not so sure about that."

Maybe it was time to be a bit more blunt, Maggie thought. "Well, Connor, I'm a part of that family life, and so is Jordan. And you know how tied up Triple I is with family. I'm not sure you can pick and choose which parts of the package you'll participate in. And that sounds like what you're trying to do."

"Maybe," he acknowledged. "And I'm not sure it's such a bad thing." Suddenly he seemed to want to end the conversation. "Listen, I've got to run. I just wanted to explain to you that if I decide not to use your idea, it's because I've got a pretty good reason for it. I'll see you at the meeting, all right?"

Maggie was frowning as she hung up. Connor's "pretty good reason" still rang false to her. And if he was still this unwilling to step into the new role he'd chosen, then she didn't have very high hopes for their future together. She was still frowning as she went upstairs to change, choosing a dressy lavender blouse and skirt with the vague thought that something elegant might offset the casualness of Connor's blue jeans.

When she arrived, she found that at least he hadn't lost his ability to surprise her. Instead of jeans, he was wearing a navy suit with an almost imperceptible pinstripe and a crisp white shirt.

"Very snazzy," she commented, as she slid into her chair.

"Thanks. I hope you don't think the tie is too loud." He brushed a finger against the muted red silk tie, and Maggie shook her head. She knew he was teasing her, yet she couldn't quite relax enough to share his joke. She was too keyed up about this meeting, wondering what Connor was planning next, and worrying about the look of strain on his handsome face.

He started the meeting on a conciliatory note, and Maggie began to breathe a little easier. "I want to start out with an explanation and an apology," he said, when all the board members were seated. "People who know me well have sometimes been heard to mutter things about bulls in china shops," he went on. "I have to admit that this past little while, there's been a certain similarity."

He'd dropped all of the abrasiveness that had gotten him into such trouble two weeks ago, Maggie noted with relief. She even saw a couple of smiles among his audience.

"I hope you'll understand that all the charging around I've done has been due to my lack of experience in this situation. As you know, it's been fifteen years since I had anything to do with Triple I, and it seems I've forgotten how things work here."

Talbot Hughes was actually nodding in agreement. Now if Connor could just go on from here...

"So I guess I need a refresher course, and it may take a little while for me to absorb it all. I'd like to ask you all to be patient while that happens."

Some of the tension was gone from Maggie's stomach, but not all. His apology had been a master stroke of diplomacy, one she wouldn't have expected from her devil-may-care gypsy. But she still needed to know what he was planning to follow up with.

At the head of the table, Connor paused, surveying the seven expectant faces. He'd decided, on his way here this evening, to take half of Maggie's good advice. She was absolutely right about the way Triple I did things, and he'd come to realize that he'd garner a lot more support with patience than with overbearing demands.

He'd decided to keep pursuing his original plan this evening, but to present it one small part at a time, in the hope that the board would go for a gradual transition where they had opposed an out-and-out revolution. But as he looked into Maggie's eyes across the long table, he found himself hesitating.

Those gold-and-hazel eyes had changed so much in his life, he thought. He loved everything about her, from the tawny curls that framed her face to her careful, considerate heart. But mostly it was the spell of her eyes that had captured him. And now, as he looked into them, he suddenly saw a truth that he'd been avoiding up till now.

She was right, he thought with a start of surprise. He drew his brows together, aware that his audience was waiting for his next words. Still he didn't speak, wrestling with this new idea.

Maggie was absolutely right about the way he'd been shying from complete involvement in the family's business and in the family itself. It was the residue of years of resentment, he knew. But now he recognized that if he was going to be a part of her life, he was going to have to stop holding himself back the way he had. The longer he locked away that most private part of himself, the less chance he had of winning Maggie Lewis. And that was the only thing that really mattered in the end.

With a start, he began to speak again, wondering how long he'd stood there thinking. To cover the lapse, he reached into the briefcase he'd brought with him, and drew out the rolled plans for his alarm system.

"I'd like to present this as a possible idea for the kind of investment I'd like to see Triple I make in the future," he told them, and then slowly and patiently, as though he was explaining it to Jordan, he went through the system he'd designed, pointing out its flexibility and the advantages it had over other systems now on the market.

As he spoke, he sensed that the idea was going over well. But the only pair of eyes he met was Maggie's, and from the dawn of sudden understanding in their depths, he knew he'd done what she'd been hoping for. She was smiling by the time he'd finished, with that serene loveliness he found so irresistible.

"We'll need to do more intensive market research, of course," he concluded, "but if you think it's worth a look, I can set that in motion before long."

"I think it's definitely worth a look," Connor's brother-in-law pronounced. "You've been too modest about your talents, Connor."

Connor was still watching Maggie, and he saw a look of amusement cross her face at the notion of Connor's being too modest about anything. "I didn't like to make it sound as though I was blowing my own horn," he said. "I want to make it clear that I'm not just using Triple I to further my own interests."

"Of course not," Caroline Lewis said quickly. "I think this is a marvelous idea. And the Blake name will give it a great deal of credibility, even though it's brand new."

Talbot Hughes was muttering, not entirely convinced. "How do we know the things will really work?" he wanted to know.

Maggie supplied the answer to that one. "Connor's Aunt Lucella had one installed, and so did several of her friends," she said. "They swear by Connor's system."

"Really? I'll have to call up Lucella," Talbot said, seemingly unaware that he was in the process of switching sides. "I knew the old girl has had bad luck with burglaries. Didn't realize young Blake here was the reason she hasn't been broken into recently."

Connor let the discussion go on until all their questions seemed to have been answered, and then he suggested putting the matter to a vote. The final tally was unanimously in favor of pursuing Connor's idea, and the meeting broke up with the air of a family gathering, instead of the armed camp it had been two weeks ago.

Maggie and Connor were the last to leave the boardroom, and after the others had gone, Connor leaned against the long table looking as though he'd just run a marathon.

"I had no idea diplomacy was so exhausting," he said, with a tired smile.

Maggie moved closer to him, playfully loosening his tie. "That's probably why so few people are really good at it," she said. "But after tonight, I'd say you have the makings of a master diplomat."

He still looked surprised at his own success. "You know, you may actually be right—about a lot of things." His smile softened as he put his arms around her.

Maggie nestled against him, feeling the familiar beating of his heart next to her ear. "What made you change your mind about the alarm system?" she asked him.

Connor took in a deep breath. He could hardly believe the moment was really here when they could look ahead into the future and see their way clear. "You did," he said simply. "I just suddenly realized how right you've been all along about the way I've avoided rejoining the family. I thought I'd done it when I took over my father's position here. But there was one more hurdle to cross, and that's the one I got over tonight."

Maggie's heart was beating fast as she listened to him. Could it really be that they'd managed to overcome everything that had kept them apart? "How does it feel to be back?" she asked softly.

He grinned at her. "Better than ever," he answered. He kissed the tawny hair on top of her head, then tilted her face up to his and kissed her lips. The scent of him and the strength of the arms that surrounded her mixed crazily with everything else Maggie was feeling.

"How would you feel about being retained permanently to keep my social life in order?" he was asking her, as he raised his lips from hers.

"What do you mean, Connor?" She never quite trusted that rogue's gleam in his eye.

"I mean will you marry me, Maggie? Be my wife." His voice cracked a little over the words, and the grin had disappeared into a look that told her exactly how much this meant to him.

Her heart was pounding hard now, but she managed a smile as she looked up into his eyes. "On one condition," she told him. She brushed the black hair back from his forehead, loving the feel of it between her fingers.

"What's the condition?" he demanded.

"That you don't get too carried away with your new respectable image," she said. "You look very dashing in that suit, Connor, but—" she loosened his tie a bit more "—just remember that the man I love is the man inside, will you?"

The kiss she gave him seemed to lay any possible doubts to rest. "I'm glad you said that," he admitted, "because it seems to me things could get pretty darn respectable all of a sudden. If I'm going to have to be the chairman of the board and president of a new company and a card-carrying member of the Blake family again—" his grin reemerged "—and if I move into that house of yours in Wellesley, and start filling up that playroom with children that belong to us instead of to other people..."

He kissed her again, and Maggie felt her senses start to overflow with the sweetness that only Connor could bring her. "Think you can handle all that and still be the gypsy I fell in love with?" she asked him, when he raised his lips from hers.

"Sure," he said, and she saw the flash of his white teeth. "And if we get out of here and go somewhere where I can get out of this suit, I'll be happy to prove it to you."

Maggie had no doubt about that, at all.

*   *   *   *   *

SILHOUETTE® Desire™

COMING NEXT MONTH

#553 HEAT WAVE—Jennifer Greene
Kat Bryant had always been cool to neighbor Mick Larson, but when she was forced to confront him about neglecting his motherless daughters sparks flew and the neighborhood really heated up!

#554 PRIVATE PRACTICE—Leslie Davis Guccione
Another Branigan-O'Connor union? According to Matthew Branigan and Bridget O'Connor—never! But when Bridget caught a glimpse of Matt's bedside manner, her knees got weak and her temperature started rising....

#555 MATCHMAKER, MATCHMAKER—Donna Carlisle
Old-fashioned chauvinist Shane Bartlett needed a wife and it was Cassie's job to find him one—an impossible task! But the search was surprisingly easy. These two opposites were the perfect match.

#556 MONTANA MAN—Jessica Barkley
He thought she was a spoiled socialite. She thought he was a jerk. Could Montana man Brock Jacoby ever tame a frisky filly like Jamaica McKenzie?

#557 THE PASSIONATE ACCOUNTANT—Sally Goldenbaum
Accountant Jane Barnett didn't like things she couldn't control—things like relationships—but Max Harris was proof that an emotional investment could yield a high return in love and happiness!

#558 RULE BREAKER—Barbara Boswell
Women never said no to rebel blue blood Rand Marshall, March's *Man of the Month*—but Jamie Saraceni did. One rejection from her and this rule breaker's bachelor days were numbered.

You'll flip . . . your pages won't!
Read paperbacks *hands-free* with

Book Mate • I

The perfect "mate" for all your romance paperbacks
Traveling • Vacationing • At Work • In Bed • Studying
• Cooking • Eating

Perfect size for all standard paperbacks, this wonderful invention makes reading a pure pleasure! Ingenious design holds paperback books OPEN and FLAT so even wind can't ruffle pages— leaves your hands free to do other things. Reinforced, wipe-clean vinyl-covered holder flexes to let you turn pages without undoing the strap . . . supports paperbacks so well, they have the strength of hardcovers!

Pages turn WITHOUT opening the strap

SEE-THROUGH STRAP

Reinforced back stays flat

Built in bookmark

BOOK MARK

BACK COVER HOLDING STRIP

10 x 7¼ opened
Snaps closed for easy carrying, too

Available now. Send your name, address, and zip code, along with a check or money order for just $5.95 + 75¢ for postage & handling (for a total of $6.70) payable to Reader Service to:

Reader Service
Bookmate Offer
901 Fuhrmann Blvd.
P.O. Box 1396
Buffalo, N.Y. 14269-1396

Offer not available in Canada
*New York and Iowa residents add appropriate sales tax

BM-G

At long last, the books you've been waiting for by one of America's top romance authors!

DIANA PALMER

DUETS

Ten years ago Diana Palmer published her very first romances. Powerful and dramatic, these gripping tales of love are everything you have come to expect from Diana Palmer.

In March, some of these titles will be available again in **DIANA PALMER DUETS**—a special three-book collection. Each book will have two wonderful stories plus an introduction by the author. You won't want to miss them!

Book 1
SWEET ENEMY
LOVE ON TRIAL

Book 2
STORM OVER THE LAKE
TO LOVE AND CHERISH

Book 3
IF WINTER COMES
NOW AND FOREVER

 *Silhouette Books*

DP-1